THE HAIR
OF
THE BEAR

CAMPFIRE YARNS AND
SHORT STORIES

By

Eric A. Bye

With Illustrations by

Tom Elisii

Eagle's View Publishing Company
6756 North Fork Road
Liberty, UT 84310
ISBN: 0-943604-30-3
Library of Congress Number - 90-82752

FIRST EDITION

This book is dedicated to my extended family: Those who are kin by birth or by buckskinning.

Publisher's Cataloging in Publication

Bye, Eric A., 1948-
  The hair of the bear : campfire yarns and short stories / by Eric A. Bye ; with illustrations by Tom Elisii. - -
  p. cm.
  ISBN 0-943604-30-3

1. Tall tales. 2. Frontier and pioneer life - Humor. 3. Humorous stories, American.
I. Title.

PS3552.Y35   817.54
                              90-82752
                              MARC

10 9 8 7 6 5 4 3 2 1

Table of Contents

Eric A. Bye

Preface

Howdy, Readers!

    You know, in the old days, folks was pretty good at yarnin'. That was before they got the notion that their entertainment had to be packaged for 'em slick and easy. Nowadays, people don't seem to tell tales like they uster, nor pick and sing so much neither, and that ain't right.

Well, I believe that I have made some fine stories for you and that you'll laff most beautifully. Why some folks has told me that these tales is more fun than a painted monkey, and pretty soon I guess you'll judge for yourself. If you like 'em, maybe you'll tell 'em around one o' your campfires.

Here's somethin' that happened to me not many moons back. You see, I was yarnin' around my campfire with a bunch of buckskinners, and folks was laffin' right proper. I sometimes had trouble makin' myself heard, though; why it sounded like the rifle range, with all the thigh-slappin' goin' on. Then right in the middle of a roarin' belly-shaker, one by one they'd stand up and go to the neighborin' camp where Abidjah Wilkins, the cooper, had his diggins. I'd see 'em in the far reaches o' the campfire light a-fussin' with somethin' for a minute or two, then back they'd come, tyin' up the sash around their blanket coats, and finish their laff harder 'n ever. I finally got so flummuxed about their leavin' at the best parts that I ast 'em what was goin' on over at the cooper's. I thought he were givin' out free Towse Lightnin', see, and I didn't want no one to get my share by mistake.

One ring-tail roarer on th' other side o' the campfire grinned so hard that his ears almost touched behind his head, and the spaces between his teeth opened up to an inch. "Haw, Haw, Haw!" he hollered. "We's just gettin' our *ribs hooped* so we don't shake our guts out laffin'! Now serve us up another tale! . . ."

Introduction

These tales are written for all who enjoy a good chuckle and a hearty adventure. Their appeal is in their outlandish humor and their reflection of the independent, adventurous lifestyle of the early American frontier. They are best when shared with family or friends, but they will also provide hours of enjoyment to those curled up at home alone. All who appreciate the American tradition of a good tall tale will be at home with these stories.

The stories are diverse in their origins. Some grew from remembered snatches of tales told to me around campfires in my boyhood. Some share the language and spirit of bona fide American frontier writings such as those of Mark Twain, the Crockett Almanacs and the personal narratives of trappers and explorers from the 19th century. A few details of plot are plucked from American legend and oral tradition, melded and amplified in new ways, consistent with what we have come to recognize as the folk process. Two or three of the tales even contain - of all things - a grain of truth! A number of the stories are, as far as I know, totally original.

If there's a thread which links these stories, it is their flavor. They are permeated with the adventurous, the outlandish, the exaggerated, the implausible, and the larger-than-life. The exaggeration, the "hugeacious" lie, possesses a strong appeal for many people. The campfire brings folks together in such a way that untruths - unacceptable in other dealings - can be relished as entertainment, free of threat. Deception and exaggeration - which are, after all, only extensions of what we respectably term as fiction - have enjoyed a long and widespread application to written and oral tales. They are amusing, and they allow the author or narrator an active interplay with the audience.

There's a lot to be said for a context which can make people feel so much at ease with one another that the lies of far-fetched yarns are accepted as the currency of entertainment. A campfire has the power to make strangers into friends, and in warm and good-natured company, one can surrender with total abandon to the entertainment value of the outlandish lie. Many of the tales that follow are of the type which have been enjoyed in camps for generations.

Most of the following tales are intentionally situated in an imprecise time period; you may read them with whatever frame of reference you choose, i.e., contemporary or 19th century. Some tales are written in correct English, and others in the uneducated, joyously reckless language we are wont to ascribe to rugged pioneer individuals. All, I hope, will succeed as stories on the printed page and as oral tales related in any setting conducive to enjoyment. The harsh and ruthless elements found in some original frontier tales and humor are, for the most part, absent from these stories. Also, for those of you who are not familiar with the terms used on the American frontier, I have written a story which explains many of them in what I hope is an entertaining manner. I highly recommend *Semi-Glossary* as the first tale you should read.

Finally, I would like to mention today's most faithful adherents of the robust frontier ethic - the buckskinners and rendezvous reenactors. In many ways, they preserve and amplify our bygone frontier culture, skills, and mannerisms; in fact, one might make the case that these people constitute a very interesting American sub-culture. They have distinctive values, trappings, nicknames and pursuits which are profoundly a part of them, and which distinguish them from most of their contemporaries. For many, the pre-1840 way of life is an alternative to the present era, which they perceive has contributed little, and taken a lot, from the quality of life. In the last quarter of the 20th century, buckskinners take refuge in the customs and practices of an America which for most people has not existed for a hundred and fifty years. The appeal of these stories to such people will be direct; but I know that others will be able to join latter-day buckskinners in an appreciation of the tales.

Whether you encounter these stories in your living room or in a primitive camp, I hope you reap some smiles from them. Perhaps they are best read in small doses, lest you become anesthetized to the laughter they can inspire. May you enjoy many more campfires; with luck, perhaps we'll even share one some time!

Semi-Glossary

Being a tale to aid the reader in understanding some of the old-time, rare, regional and low-falutin' words (in bold type)   which appear in subsequent stories.

One of my ancestors, great-great-great-great-grandad Zadock, was a member of Ashley's original party that left St. Lou in 1822. He'd responded to the famous help-wanted ad that changed the course of western history, and stayed in the wilderness for about two-score years all told. He was a flinty adventurer who survived a passel of hair-raising scrapes. I have in my possession Zadock's **fusil** - a flintlock smoothbore Northwest trade gun with the sitting fox stamped on the lock and barrel - and his **possibles**, consisting of all the accoutrements needed to load, shoot and maintain his firearm: horn, pouch, bullet mold and so forth. I will share with you an interview done by a newspaper reporter near the end of Zadock's life. The interview was conducted as part of the centennial celebrations of Castor, Idaho, where Zadock was one of the early settlers. There he worked for years as a **cooper** in his small wood shop, supplying barrels and casks to his neighbors and to emigrants headed farther west. The reporter, a Mr. Bezaleel Craddock, notes that my ancestor was of rather short stature, with thin white hair, erect posture and clear eye. He had a colorful manner of speaking which the reporter tried to preserve in his transcription of the interview. From time to time, Zadock took a pull from a jug containing some of his special corn squeezings (his personal supply of **'shine** which he referred to as **arwerdenty** and **Towse**

Lightin') flavored with a couple of beaver castors. The following adventures relate to my ancestor's musket and reveal some of his spunk, if not his visionary powers. Here is a portion of the interview as recorded nearly verbatim by the reporter:

"You know young feller, I natcherly talks the way I learned in the wilderness, so ever' time I come to somethin' you don't catch on to, why you just look up and I'll try to explain, deal? I guess before we're done, you'll come to see that this ol' **dog-face** - uh, that's what the Injuns called us bearded white trappers - was one o' the shootin'est, ridin'est and trappin'est critters in the hills. This ol' **hiveranno** had the **Hair of the Bear** in him, he did, and he **seen the lizard and the elephant**. (Transcribers note: The narrator means he had traveled west, endured hardships and wintered over in the wilderness). We'd started off on our expedition pretty good and made many a **plew** - beaver pelts, you know - but after a while, things started to go sour. Finally, after a few months o' ramshackin' around the woods and hills without finding much sign o' beaver - them durned Hudson's Bay bandits had been under orders to trap out all the streams and lakes so the Americans would skedaddle from what they considered to be their territory - we concluded to split up and explore for better trappin' grounds. Lord! How you do make that quill fly! I **swan** - I mean I swear - I never seen a body scribble so fast! Anyway, most o' the guys went off by pairs. But I was off doin' my business in the bushes when the choosin' was takin' place, and since there was an uneven number o' skinners in the party, I ended up as a solo leftover.

"That didn't bother me none, and I turned down offers to join other groups as a third man. Truth to tell,

I was gettin' tired o' society and didn't mind the prospect o' headin' out for a couple o' weeks o' scoutin' **aux ailments du pays** (that be French talk for livin' off the land, foragin' and huntin' for yer grub; you see, sometimes we picked up expressions from the Canadian **coureurs des bois** or wood runners in our party). Anyway, with partin' words o' "Keep yer eyes skinned", "Watch yer topknot" and "Keep yer powder dry", we all lit out to diff'rent points on the compass. The **boosh-way** (that be Mr. Ashley, our head honcho) hollers good luck to us and promises a feast o' boudins to the trappers that keeps their hair and returns with news o' beaver aplenty. Oh - you be wonderin' what in Tunket them **boudins** is - well, see, they's stuffed buffler intestines roasted on a campfire till they's hot and drippin' with juice - ain't no better fare in the mountains nor on the prairie neither, my friend.

"Well, I'd been on the trail for a couple sleeps when I had to cross this broad river. I'd seen tracks in the mud that told of a whole **cavvyard** - must have been a half dozen or more - o' Bugs' Boys - that's what we called hostile warriors, see. It was plain that there was a war party skulkin' about hopin' to **count some coup**. That means scorin' on an enemy, like bein' the first to touch him in battle. Whew! It's a mite tiresome explainin' ever'thing like this, but it seems you and I hardly talk the same lingo. Anyhow, I knew I had to keep my eye on the ridgeline or I might meet some trouble. There was a tarnal heavy rain pourin' down as my mount and I slid into the current at what appeared to be a ford. I had stuck the quill of a feather into the vent of my fusil and tied on my **cow's knee** to keep my charge from wettin'. (Transcriber's note: The narrator had used a feather to plug the flash-hole of his flintlock and tied a leather cover over the lock area to keep the rain from spoiling the shot in his rifle). I had checked around from the safety of a grove o' cottonwoods before settin' out across the river and didn't see no signs o' hostiles. Bein' alone, I'd 'a rather met up with a **lucivee** or a **razor-shins** or a **Windigo** or some other o' them hellacious monsters they tells about in the North Woods. But I figgered that war party might lay low anyway, since in that wet weather, their sinew-backed bows and their bow strings would be all **catawampus** - I mean discombobulated, softened up too much to work right, see?

"Well, I'll be dipped in dung if right in mid-stream, just when my hoss was havin' his feet swept out from under him, there didn't come a tarnacious **carrumux** on the shore behind me: a thunderin' and a splashin' and a squawkin' like the hinges o' Hell. Bugs' Boys had found me, see, and was chargin' into the water. I nearly fell into the drink and succeeded in plungin' my **fusil** - or musket- into the water past the lock as I struggled to stay mounted. My hoss and I was the first to light on the opposite bank, and we cut dirt lickity-clippity.

"I figgered it was useless to try a shot after that dunkin', but I pulled the quill out o' the touch hole and managed to prime the piece and aim as I twisted in the saddle. Klatch-fssssss-boom! Ol' Thunderclap hung fire, but by Tunket, she roared and threw her charge o' buck and ball, and them braves scattered like leaves! I whooped with joy when I felt the **comb** o' that buttstock recoil into my cheek. From the look o' things I figgered they was young bucks out to prove 'emselves. I **snum** - I mean I declare - I **vum**, I **vummy**, them words is all the same, you know - I was mighty impressed that my musket shot after such a drenchin'. I thought a lot about that wet-weather shot and concluded I owed it to my precautions, and to the fact that I always used a real tight-patched ball that would 'a kept the water from enterin' the charge from the muzzle. That's a lesson that wasn't lost on this child.

"I kept my lookers skinned on my back trail for a day or so, but didn't see no more sign o' trouble. Then one night after dark, I'd just finished eatin' a mess o' fish and **galette** - that's a kind o' bread we'd cook in a fry pan, 'bout as thick as a buffler chip, but good eatin' - and had stepped to the river's edge to clean my pan. Like a durned **mangeur de lard** - that be French talk for pork eater or greenhorn, like a **cheechako**, as some say - I'd left my fusil in camp, but at least I had my belt pistol and horn and possibles on me. Before I knew it, a half-dozen thievin' copper-skinned rascals stole out o' the shadders and made off with my mount and everythin' in camp. I fired my pistol as they pulled foot, but never touched 'em. I yelled **Peste!, Sacre!** and all the other curses I knew, and in my frustration, I threw down my **tuque** (this here Canadian-type floppy hat) and practically stomped it to flinderations.

"You can imagine I felt mighty **exflunctificated** - plum sick to death - over losin' ever'thin' like that. I spent the night in the cottonwoods and in the mornin' I started back mounted on nothin' but my mockersons. I figgered to stick to the river, since it would lead me in the right direction. Long as I didn't meet big trouble in the shape of another war party or **Ol' Ephraim** - that's what we called Grizz or grizzle b'ars - I hoped I could join my companyeros in less'n a week o' travel.

"Long about dusk on my first day on the trail, I peered over a rise and spied a canoe full of Injuns slicin' through the river. They was far enough away so I couldn't see if they was the same bunch that had raided my camp, but I sot my thinker to work and made a plan.

There was a snag that stuck out into the current, and I eased out into the water behind it, out o' sight o' the braves in the canoe. I primed my pistol, which was loaded with the same tight ball and patch combination that had saved my bacon before, felt for the **Green River** knife on my belt, and waited for my chance. Alright, you devils, I thought to myself, we'll see whose **medicine shines** tonight. Yes sir, we'll just see who comes out on top o' this tussle!

"When the canoe was almost across from me, I eased out farther into the current. I held my primed pistol out of the water as I swam with my free hand. My timing was just right, for in a minute, I pulled just ahead of the canoe, unrecognized in the near darkness. I rolled onto my back, frog-kicking silently under the surface with my feet, and unsheathed my Green River in case I needed it. I held the pistol right in front of my face so I could draw a bead on the lead man in such a way that a close shot might pass through more than one. Then with my teeth I pulled the quill from the flash-hole of my pistol. I screeched like a gelded **painter** - uh, wild-cat or cougar, you'd say - "You thievin' varmints! I come to claim my plunder!" I fired my pistol, which sparked and fizzed like a slow fuse before the main charge went. Why, I could 'a caught and fried a fish in the time it took for that piece to fire. But I got the desired effect, for at the sight of that dog-faced fire-spittin' water monster, the braves dropped everything and pitched over the gunnels with a shriek. They upset the canoe, but I was able to right it and keep on travelin' downstream with a paddle I rescued from the swim. Tied to the thwart with a piece o' rawhide thong so it wouldn't be lost in a swampin' was this here fine chief's grade fusil. Lookat this inlay, and the carvin' and engravin'! I must 'a dunked somebody important. You see, that wasn't the same party that had plundered my camp, and I was still out a horse; but by Tunket I'd lost an ordinary trade musket and ended up with a better one, and the same caliber. I paddled all night and rested by day for safety, and after a couple days, I met up with some of my companyeros. They'd had a scrape with the thieves I'd met and reconfiscated all my plunder, plus some o' theirs. So we finished the trip in good shape and met Mr. Ashley, who made good on his word by treatin' us to a fine roast on the prairie. Some of the fellers had found rich trappin' streams, and we spent a bounteous season wadin' and harvestin' plews. And that's history, my friend.

"I've often thought o' how them flintlocks fired under wet conditions and nevermore felt **squamptious** - uh, uncomfortable, that is - about takin' 'em out in all types o' weather. You just gotta know how to load 'em and keep 'em dry. Why, I'll wager my **gage d'amour** here, this little pouch hangin' around my neck where I keep my 'baccy and clay pipe, that these new-fangled caplock guns won't last long. Heck, they's nothin' but a fad. Mark my word!"

Eric A. Bye

CHECKMATE

I've got the hair of the bear and the spleen of the wolverine in me. I've hunted high and low for bear in these Green Mountains. I've had close scrapes before and taken my share of game, too. But about two moons back I had a run-in that made me think about hanging up my gun and possibles for good. You see, when you're after the biggest, meanest bruin in creation you must go afield with the best weapon and the strongest medicine in the world: the conviction that you are an invincible force and *the* critter in all the wilderness to beat. If you ever lose the strength that comes of that belief, you're a gone beaver when you go against dangerous game.

You know, I've become a crack shot with my front loader by sending many tons of lead after stationary targets at long distances. After years of practice and bushels of flints, I have become an expert at hitting such long-range targets. Therefore, it was with the utmost confidence that I set out in pursuit of a clever bruin that had ravaged a family's intended supply of pork down at the settlements. The critter had come back a couple of nights in a row to carry off more hogs, and he had escaped with more plunder each time. He didn't care about fences, for he just plowed through them. The last time he visited, the settler might have winged him with a hasty shot. Since the bear was big and ugly and maybe wounded, and since the settler didn't have a proper bear gun, he asked me to track him and dispatch him.

I'd had a couple of miles of easy tracking, for the bear left big tracks and lots of debris behind. But at one point, as the trail passed over a broad and trackless ledge with huge boulders and windfalls scattered around, I really had to study hard to find sign. I had knelt and was peering at the ground, motionless, when without warning, and quicker than a hammer-fall, the malicious bruin I sought pounced mightily from behind a deadfall. His roar echoed from the surrounding hills, and as he sailed through the air at me his fetid breath was like the wind from the gates of Hell. I scarcely had time to raise and fire - and by dismal luck I missed clean! Imagine my astonishment as the bear, whose adrenalin-fired rage had caused him to miscalculate the distance, sailed clear over my head and landed fifteen feet behind me! He instantly wheeled about in a cyclone of leaves and twigs and pounced at me again as I hastily yanked my pistol and fired a second time - missing, confound it all!, as ineptly as in the first attempt. The monster again landed five paces beyond me, and I figured I was a gone beaver this time. With an empty rifle and nothing but my belt knife for defense, I drew the blade and wheeled to face the monster; but to my relief, the bear continued through the thicket, leaving me with the narrowest escape of my life and plenty of food for thought concerning my nearly fatal miss on such a critical target.

Before you conclude that this narrow brush with death is what caused me to consider hanging up my shooting gear, I must stress that I am not of such a fearful nature. Rather, that experience merely served to increase my fervor in hunting the bear, but with one major change in tactics.

For you see, it became clear to me that I had failed at the critical moment because I had trained only on stationary targets at long ranges. In order to prepare for the kind of shot which had presented itself, I determined that I needed to practice shooting *moving* targets at *close* range. I began in earnest, and soon was able to consistently hit a wood chip thrown into the air. My confidence restored, I felt ready to fulfill my promise to the settler and even the score with the outlaw bear.

I was on his trail once again and was approaching the scene of my first blood-curdling encounter. I was doubly alert and very apprehensive about repeating the previous experience. As I neared the ledge, I was puzzled to hear a series of roars followed immediately by a vicious crashing and a gnashing of teeth. This strange sound was repeated about every thirty seconds. You can imagine my astonishment when I crested a rise and beheld - even more immense and ferocious than my first glimpse had indicated - the selfsame bruin that had nearly devoured me a short time previous.

The truth is, compadres, that the bear was intently practicing *short jumps* at a man-sized log which he was using as a *stationary* target! He pounced on it with all his weight and bit off limbs and raked it with his claws and shook it in his mouth until the bark and splinters fairly flew! I turned and tiptoed out of the woods the same way I'd come in. Now I suspect that my settler friend and the bear are both waiting for me to finish my task; but as far as I'm concerned, they can keep waiting, and the bear can help himself to as much pork as he'd like.

My Disagreement With A Sarpent

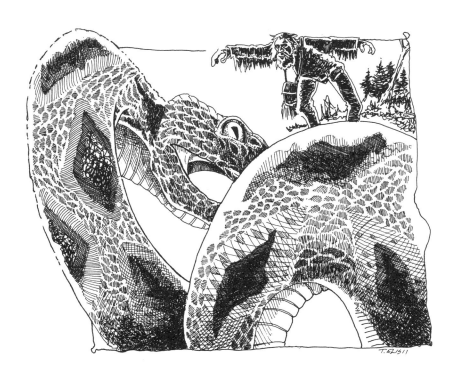

My nearest neighbor, five miles away, fell so catawampusly exflunctificated with th'epizootic that he took to his bed and sent word with a passing hunter that he couldn't do chores. I pulled foot for his diggin's so I could milk the cow and feed the chickens for him. But since I had a nation o' chores to do at my own cabin- I was fixin' fence around the upper garden at the time - I scallyhooted back home jest as soon as I was done. I was in such a tear to get back that I cut through the woods on the shortest line 'twixt his cabin and mine. I had to go right through where the ledges meets the swamp; and since I was thinkin' about my work and wasn't really huntin' for nothin', ol' Kildeer wasn't even loaded. I might not even 'a' brought her just to go do chores for a neighbor, but you know I just don't feel dressed without a rifle in my hand.

Anyway, as I stepped by the foot o' the ledges, I heerd a rattlin' like somebody shakin' the bones at a barn dance. I looked up and right there, quoiled around the limb o' this big oak tree, was the most monstratious rattle-sarpent I ever seed. He opened his mouth so wide I could see four feet down his gullet, and I swan I fairly swooned on his putrid breath. I reached quick for my powder and balls, but the way he reared up to strike, I could see I would never get a charge in Kildeer. That was sartinly a most constarnacious perdicament, for wherever I put foot I was still in his range. I could tell he didn't want me movin' too quick, but I hit on an ideer that maybe I could outsmart him if I moved slow and deliberate. Sure enough, as I moved forward, his head moved forward; I stepped slow to the left, and he moved to the left; I eased myself one step back - as far as the ledge allowed - and sure enough, his head followed. So I says to myself, I'll get out of this stew shortly; jest watch this, Mr. Sarpent! And, thinkin' back to the days when I was a salt plowin' the briny ocean, I resolved to put some of my knot-tyin' know-how to use. I moved real cautious-like two steps right. He rattle out a warnin', but he follow. So I steps up on a rock behind me, and up he come; then I steps forward and down, then in a circle, and Snake do the same. I cuts another curlycue or two and Snake tags along, crossin' over hisself and tuckin' through a loop. Why, a body'd 'a' thought we was dancin', with that snake followin' my lead so smooth and true. So at the last instant, I make a quick jump back; Snake shoots his head straight out to strike, cinchin' himself down in a perfect bowline tight around that oak limb! I'm already out o' strikin' distance, and he's tied right proper! The color riz up in his face, and he hollered most hidjusly and screeched like a steam boiler, so I decide to cut dirt for home. Halfway back, though, I think to myself, what if I have to help with my neighbor's chores again tomorrow? I'll have to pass through that spot agin, but it'll be a pleasanter walk without that scaly turn-stile. So I resolved to do the manly thing and go back to do mortal combat with the sarpent.

I charged my rifle and sneaked back to the spot by a different trail just to play it safe. I wish to be stung to death by no-seeums if this ain't true. That oak tree was dead and withered, lyin' on the ground as limp as a biled beet green, except the trunk were swollen and black in several places where the monster had punctu-rated it with his fangs. I see where a branch had been ripped off and drug in the direction I had gone earlier, so I knowed the viper was still tied. He was trailin' me, only he couldn't go too fast on account o' his unaccus-tomed walkin' stick. So I backtrailed until, sure enough, I spied the infidel lyin' in ambush for me. That weren't the day for his medicine to shine, though, for I out-sneaked him and drew a bead on his head with a load of buck and ball. My shot took him in the eye and spoiled his whole day. Mr. Sarpent scream once more and writhe most beautifully for five minutes before headin' to his final penalty. I gutted him on the spot, and the critter were so long I had to stop and whet my butcher knife three times. As I dragged him home, he straightened out and rigger-mortise sot in. So's to make up for lost time, I used him as the top rail on my garden fence, and the bugger spanned three posts. And you know, I ain't had nary a varmint o' any kind around my garden since.

A Strong Attraction

Four of us were hunting in unfamiliar country. We all rode good mounts and carried our supplies on a cavvyard of sturdy pack animals. Two days into the wilderness, our compasses began to act strangely, pointing straight to the setting sun! We wanted to head west anyway, and knew we could trust our directions by the sun. So we continued our hunt with scarcely another thought about the odd behavior of our compasses - at least for a time.

A few nights later in camp, we were throwing the tomahawk for practice. Though the air was calm, we kept missing the mark. The 'hawks described a strange curve in the air and careened wildly to slap the target broadside or miss it wide, always on the same side.

The following day, we found it hard to ride in a straight line across a flat plain. Try as we might, we always wandered a few degrees off our mark. In particular, the pack horse carrying the cookware and fire irons had to be continually hauled back into line with the others. The streams we crossed became increasingly unsavory, running thick and orange in color. We were beginning to feel a little uneasy in that peculiar country. That night we set up camp a few miles from a high mountain whose bare peak showed red in the late sun.

I left camp on horseback to get some game for supper. I managed to shoot a few squirrels, but as I sighted, my hold was strangely unsteady. I felt that I was resisting some unseen force which caused my rifle to shun the target. I had a mighty queersome feeling, for I sensed I was in the presence of some strong medicine. My mount felt it, too, since he swung his shod hooves in an awkward way when he walked and acted mighty skittish. As we headed back to camp, the hackles on my neck bristled and I couldn't resist casting a couple of uneasy glances over my shoulder.

Upon my return, I discovered my companyeros in a state of great consternation. There was talk of haunts and poltergeists. One hivernant had set a tin cup of hot coffee on his knee by the campfire and it had spontaneously - deliberately, it seemed - keeled over and spilled down his leggins. An iron spoon set in a bowl of soup moved around the edge of the bowl by itself so that it always pointed in the same direction. Another hunter had nearly chopped his foot while trying to split wood for the fire, for he couldn't strike the mark with his axe. Talk favored breaking camp and high-tailing it out of the valley. But I knew there had to be a logical explanation for the odd occurrences. Using soup spoons and compasses, I determined that everything pointed to the summit of the rust-colored mountain visible not far off, and I concluded that it was loaded with magnetic deposits. The rusty streams in the area supported my claim that the peak - thereafter known to us as Magneto Mountain - contained plenty of iron.

I convinced my companyeros that we were witnessing a logical phenomenon and not bad medicine. We remained in camp that night and resolved to scale the Mountain the next day to satisfy our curiosity.

Upon setting out for the peak, we consciously took off and left in camp all the iron and steel we had - knives, guns, tomahawks, fire kits, spurs, tools, and so forth. We left one man to guard the camp and hiked to the base of the mountain. There we found several perfectly parallel streams precisely the same distance from one another - about eighteen inches - that ran down together straight from the summit. We eventually followed these clear to the peak, where we found all manner of iron implements. At the head of those streams was an old farm plow that had been drawn for miles up the mountain by magnetic force. The furrows it created had turned into streams for the runoff.

We noticed that all the trees we passed on the way to the summit leaned toward the peak. Deadfalls landed only uphill; most were uprooted, and had begun a creeping ascent of the mountain. Inch by inch, the trunks were being drawn up the mountainside, leaving a shallow trough which connected them to the craters which had once been their stand. One climber who sat on such a log to take a rest could actually feel it move beneath him and concluded that if a body had more time than energy, he could even ride the log to the top of the mountain. Of course these trees were ironwoods. Generation after generation of seeds were sucked to the ground with such force that they immediately imbedded themselves in the soil and sprouted.

Close to the summit, we found the remains of a wagon loaded with hardware: anvils, tools, gun parts, and trade axes, now coated with heavy rust. Skeletons of horses remained in the rotted harness, and the wear on their bones indicated that they'd been dragged up the mountain by the wagonload of iron. We also found a steel strongbox frozen tight to the side of a rock face. For all we knew it contained a fortune, and you can bet we tried everything to get into it. Sledge hammers, drills, wedges, pry bars, axes - all the rusty tools we could scrounge from the wreckage - were of no avail. Short of blasting the safe apart with dynamite, we had no hope of discovering its contents. So, dejectedly, we abandoned the project and continued exploring.

At the summit, we gazed down the opposite slope of the mountain and saw a lake of rusty water several hundred feet below. It lay on a forty-five degree slope and a stream poured out of its uphill end to flow over the peak and down the furrows we'd followed in our ascent.

Momentarily a noise rang out like a rifle shot and we all scrambled for cover. We were totally unarmed and lay low for a minute until we heard our camp guard halloo a mere fifty yards away. We answered his call and came out into the open.

He explained that his curiosity had won out and he wanted to see the summit for himself. He figured he could find the most direct route to the top by rolling a tin cup uphill from the base of the mountain. The higher he hiked, the faster the cup rolled, until he couldn't keep up with it any longer. At the end, it fairly flew away. "And there it is now," he remarked. And we saw the remains of his cup flattened against a vertical cliff face where it was stuck fast. It looked like a coin flattened on the rails by the Iron Horse. Its impact made the noise we'd mistaken for a gunshot.

As we took a final look around, one partner in particular seemed to be taking careful inventory of the old implements and tools stuck to the rock surfaces. We returned to camp, retrieved our gear, and completed our hunt.

While in camp, we made an astonishing discovery. Earlier I had gone to one of the streams for a bucket of water to keep by the campfire. It remained in the sun all day while we were out exploring, and upon our return we found that under the evaporating power of the sun, the rusty water had condensed to form an iron plug that filled the bottom half of the bucket. We subsequently experimented by evaporating tin cups of water to form good quality iron ingots. And we found that by pouring a few drops into our moulds, we could cast usable bullets and shot. I was struck by the commercial possibilities of this discovery, for here one could operate a foundry with no equipment other than a few moulds, and I mentally began calculations to account for the shrinkage due to evaporation.

About a month later, back at the settlements, I learned that my partner who'd seemed so interested in all the ironware at the top of Magneto Mountain had concluded a mighty favorable business deal. Seems that he'd sold - sight unseen - the strong box and wagon load of old tools, parts and farm implements to an antique dealer from down country who'd agreed to come and pick up the whole lot. Why, we even had a chance to meet the fellow, for when he came to get his goods, our buddy was nowhere to be found and the flatlander sought us out. I can't say he was too civil, either. He mentioned something about presenting our partner with a big suit, but I told him he could save his money, for none of us had any use for fancy clothes.

You see, the businessman had speculated on the contents of that safe and paid a king's ransom for it. Well, when he blasted it apart to get to the contents, you know what he found? Nothing but a manufacturer's warranty and an old yellowed booklet of operating instructions! Why, that safe was brand new and on its way to its first owner when it got sidetracked to the top of Magneto Mountain. It never had a chance to hold a penny, and worse yet, it caused a bundle of that speculator's money to disappear! I guess I can understand why he got his tail in a knot!

Outfoxed

I had just discovered huge bear tracks not far from my cabin and was in relentless, daily pursuit of the critter that had left them behind. They were distinctive not only because of their astonishing size but also because of a large scar on one pad of the right forepaw. I knew that those tracks were the link between a one-of-a-kind trophy bruin and me; and by dint of stealth, experience, and persistence, I would shorten the distance between us, much as one reels in a fish. I felt confident and inexorable.

Now, I should explain that I am a purist and perfectionist. I mean to get my game just as any serious hunter does, but that has to be accomplished in the *right* way for me, or I'll have none of it. That ethic has required refining my skills over the years, and giving the quarry every reasonable advantage to keep the contest challenging in light of my ever-increasing expertise. I allow myself only one shot, and my choice of a long arm is a 58 caliber flintlock smoothbore. I hunt alone and follow a single track relentlessly. I hunt in the primitive way because I want success to be due to my prowess in the wilderness rather than due to blind luck or unfair technological advantages. Finally, my eventual shot must be not only certain, but as *demanding* as possible. I never waver from these standards, and I've enjoyed abundant success - except in one instance when the quarry refused to play by the same rules.

One frigid night as I sat drowsily before a fire in my log hut, dreamily plotting the morning's strategy, I was startled to hear a thumping and scratching at the rough door. Disbelieving the presence of other humans, I none the less called out for the visitor to identify himself. I thought I heard a voice in reply, and still not knowing if I was dreaming or waking, I opened the door a crack to peer into the night. Instantly, a large, rank black form crowded past me into my cabin and took a place near the fire.

My rifle was out of reach beyond the intruder, whom I recognized as a tremendous black bear! In my confusion, I was about to bolt through the door into the frozen blackness, when I was checked by a gruff voice from the hearth which commanded: "Pilgrim! Come and talk!"

Unable to disobey, I moved like a sleepwalker toward the hearth. My head swam as I sank disbelieving onto a wooden bench. The bear spoke rationally and clearly enjoyed the upper hand on me as I repeatedly blinked in disbelief and ricocheted back and forth between illusion and reality.

"Your prowess as a bear-slayer is proverbial throughout the forest kingdom," began the bear. Disoriented though I was, I was gratified by his preamble and acknowledged the compliment with an involuntary smile. "We bears drew straws to determine which of us would be sacrificed this season, and I lost. You have been on my trail for several days. I know it's only a matter of time before my fate is consummated, so I resolved to do what no other bear has done in many millennia: confront the hunter in his den and enjoy a brief but exalted reputation for courage among my ursine peers. In so doing, I must ask for a small object as proof of this visit, as no other bear would accompany me as witness."

I considered that there was no more telling proof of his visit, or better omen of its eventual outcome, than an unfired .58 round ball, which he accepted with gratitude tinged with uneasiness. "But how did you know," I asked him, "that I wouldn't shoot you here in my cabin?"

"I was counting on your confusion and wonderment to dissuade you from an untimely consummation of the deed. Now if you please, tell me a little about your hunting so that I can further substantiate my story with information straight from the hunter's mouth."

I'm not a little proud of my accomplishments as a game-getter, and the bruin's evident admiration of my skill may have excited my ego a bit. I have, frankly, received many testimonials of my skills from hundreds of intimate friends who are among the most accomplished hunters on the continent; but after all they are mere intruders and part-timers in the wilderness. Here, on the other hand, was an homage paid to my hunting prowess by none other than a prince of the wilderness, unique in his size, experience, and intelligence. I explained to him my views and meticulousness much as I did to you at the start of this account. In so stressing my perfectionist nature, I unsuspectingly tipped my hand; and as I will presently relate, that insight was not lost on my guest.

Shortly, the bear thanked me and rose to leave. At the door, he held up his rifle bullet to examine it in the light from the fireplace, and I noticed the already familiar scar on the pad of his forepaw. Then he clapped me smartly on the shoulder and slipped out into the darkness. As the heavy churning of his footsteps in the frozen leaves grew fainter, I clutched the door jamb and considered that a four-legged had just figuratively and in fact counted coup on me.

I tossed and turned all night and still couldn't separate illusion from fact. But I was up before dawn and clear-headed with the imperative of the day's hunt. Instantly, I picked up the tracks outside my door and followed them for miles through swamps and thickets and ridges and ledges. That was just as I liked it: the brute was leading me on a hard chase that let me savor the pursuit.

Around dusk, I sensed that I was getting close. My pulse quickened as I checked my priming powder, for I felt that circumstances were favorable and that I was destined to consummate the hunt precisely as I required.

Momentarily the undergrowth opened into a clearing. A scant hundred feet away was my bear standing broadside, immobile, on top of a blowdown that raised him above all intervening brush. My smoothbore was halfway to my shoulder when an internal alarm sounded: "Hold it! This is too easy!" Hoping to force at least a running shot, I yelled at the bear, who parted his chops and grunted once, but refused to budge. I threw a rock at him and walked into the clearing. Still the old boar held his ground. I stamped, cursed him and his ancestors, waved my arms, and finally fired my one shot over his back in frustration. It was no use; he had beaten me; he would never allow the kind of triumph I required.

My head was swimming as I sat down heavily. The bear stalked away with nary a backward glance. Later I regained my senses and walked to the blowdown where the bear had perched, hoping to discover that only my fatigue and my obsession had caused me to imagine the bear. But there by the blowdown, in the first track of a scarred forepaw, lay an unfired .58 roundball.

Fresh Bait

I was fishin' from the shore amongst the weeds of the setback and had just lost my last piece of bait. The greedy lunker gave a yank and raised such a carrumux on the surface of the water that I jerked awake from a snooze and dropped my fishin' cane into the water; I would have lost it, too, if he'd been hooked proper. Now where in Tunket was I to get another piece of bait? A frog swimmin' on the surface of the water a short distance from shore caught my eye. Instantly there was a loud *slurp* and the frog vanished amidst a swirl of fins and a whirlpool that opened a funnel clean to the bottom of the drink! "Great earth and seas!" I hollered, all primed-in-the-pan ready to land a champeen fish. He was still there just a rod's length from me, and I didn't have a shred of bait. I knew that I needed a frog and that nothin' else would shine, so I called out to that fish, "Stay close, amigo, dessert's a-comin'!" and rushed off to find me a juicy croaker.

I memorized the spot where I last saw the fish and hurried up and down the banks lookin' for any ol' frog, toad, peeper, or pollywog, live or dead. You know, there wasn't one to be found nowheres. Why I would 'a paid a dollar for a frog! I was afeared to get too far away from the spot where I'd last seen the fish and was at my wit's end for a frog, when up to the shore swum sideways one o' them inseedious-lookin' copper-mouth rattle moccasins with a nice juicy croaker in his mouth. Another minute and that frog'd be a goner, and I needed him. Now if you've never tried to trick supper away from a pizenous snake before, you can't scarcely imagine the perdickamint I was in. Well, I'll try this, I says to myself, reachin' for my hip flask real slow so's not to rile Mr. Sarpent. Then plip-plop I dribbles two or three drops of my prime Eagle Sweat corn squeezin's onto that snake's nose. He squinch up his eyes real tight and straightaway he spit that croaker out whole! Out come his crimson tongue several times, and then back into the water he slinks. I pick up the frog and put him on the hook and commence to fish in earnest for the big one.

I'd made a couple o' casts, when what do I see but that same snake come slidin' up to my feet again with two frogs in his mouth! The sly critter had come back for a double shot! He helped me several more times, too, always bringin' frogs to pay for his drinks. And when I caught that big lunker, I treated my long slender friend to a free round and a left-over frog. And you know what? Them snakes slithers all crooked when they're sober; but after bringin' my bait and gettin' paid, my helper swum straight as an arrer.

Uncle Eef's Rifle

My uncle Eef Gump, whom I admired more than anyone in the world, enjoyed a reputation as a peerless hunter and flintlock marksman. I wanted to learn to shoot as well as he, so I approached him to learn what I could.

"I suppose you practice every day to keep your eye sharp," I began. Uncle Eef was slow to take the bait. He was initially reluctant to share his secrets, but after a few minutes' resistance he began to soften.

"I wouldn't tell this to jest *anyone*, but since one day you may own my rifle-," and here I really sat up and took notice, "you mought's well know. But if'n yer smart, you'll keep what I'm about to tell ye tight under yer hat."

"You know, I really don't practice much a-tall. Sure, when I were your age, I shot hard and learned the basics, but now I don't scarcely need to practice. Truth to tell, the secret's partly in the technique and partly in the gun. See, when I made the piece many year ago, I spent all my plews on th' barrel. Got me the best tapered-and-flared one with a choke-bore and hand-cut, hand-lapped riflin'. After buyin' that, I kinda had to skimp on the lock, and that jest aren't up to snuff, so much the pity. So the ignition's a nation slower'n what most folks is uster. I don't guess my home-made powder helps none either. But I's shot her so much that it's normal to me and it don't bother none, long's I don't disremember to foller through right proper." I thought I already knew everything about follow-through; so far I judged I hadn't gleaned any priceless bits of wisdom and eagerly awaited more. Uncle comprehended my questioning glance and reached to hand me the long-barreled flinter. "Here, try this for size," he winked.

I noted instantly how the fingerbow of the trigger guard and the swelling in the forestock at the rear ramrod pipe seemed made for my hands. Uncle and I are about the same build, and the drop in the comb was just right for me. As I made to shoulder the piece, it fairly jumped into position, almost of its own accord. "By Tunket," I exclaimed, "It almost seems alive!" I sighted a moment along the barrel, aiming at a fly on the opposite wall of Uncle's cabin. The rifle never wavered; the balance was so perfect that holding it on target was effortless. As I shouldered the rifle, it seemed to embrace me. "Why, this rifle hangs so natural and steady," I marveled, "that I feel like I could hold it all day. I never before felt a rifle that hung so solid and comfortable."

"You're right, and I snum you never will feel another one. That rifle's got powerful medicine, and I'll never part with her while I still draw breath. I'll tell you an experience I had with her that proves her worth. You ain't shot her yet, so keep in mind what I said earlier about her bein' slow to fire; but now you know how natural she *hangs* and *points.* Yessir! How she does hang *solid!*"

Uncle Eef's rocker creaked as he leaned back. His gaze moved beyond me and his eyes narrowed as he focused on the past. "You see, I had gone a-huntin' deer early o' one mornin' and had walked a couple hundred yards from my cabin here. I was headin' up the ol' woods lane to see if'n I could pick up a track where one o' them wily devils had crossed. As luck would have it, before I'd gone too far I spotted a spikehorn asleep in his bed. 'This is a promisin' start,' I thought to myself as I raised to fire. I took careful aim and pulled the trigger. At the same time I heard the KLATCH of the hammer, all kinds o' horrified screams o' 'FIRE !' broke out o' the clearin' behind me. I knew my wife and children weren't hollerin' for me to shoot, and that the cabin were burnin'; so in an instant, I just let go o' the rifle - like that! - and dropped my possibles and bolted home empty handed. Well, the cabin still stands, so you might guess it were just our yearly chimbly fire, and after a few minutes we had everything under control and Beulah finished cookin' up breakfast. I were so relieved that we'd saved the cabin again that I stayed for a bite o' breakfast, and then, much refreshed, I headed back to the woods to see if I could locate some venison and salvage the hunt.

"I returned to the spot where I'd stood to shoot in order to retrieve my rifle and possibles. Naturally, I expected to find everythin' in a jumble on the ground. My possibles were right where I expected, but my rifle wasn't there. Imagine my amazement when I discovered the rifle still hangin' motionless in the air five feet off the ground. I heard the primin' in the pan still fizzlin' away, so I stepped behind the rifle and put my hands on her just in time to take the recoil and harvest a fine buck."

I hardly dared to doubt Uncle Eef's word, so I tempered my skepticism. "Now Uncle, I allow that this rifle hangs steady; but you don't expect me to believe that spikehorn was dumb enough to stay in his bed without stirring when the hollerin' started and you ran home to douse a fire!"

"Of course not! That deer was no fool. He got up and ran away when I did. But while I was gone, the rifle spotted another, bigger buck passin' through and picked up on *him*! That's the one I bagged and them's his antlers over the door. Now ain't that some rifle," he grinned. "I wouldn't trade her for all the gold in California!"

How I Acted In My Own Defense

April 1, 1825
Boonesboro, Kentucky

Mr. Elkanah Partridge
Rocky Mountain Fur Company
Western Territories

Dear Cousin Elkanah,
        I am writing you in the hope that some fellow
trapper in your camp will be able to read you this letter.
I imagine that in your isolation from the comforts of
civilization you must fairly crave news from the settlements. Furthermore, I have just had such an extraor-
dinary experience that I must communicate it to someone, or I will burst. You are the first person to whom
I have written of this adventure, for I feel that of all my
friends and family, you will have the readiest appreciation of its singular nature. And lastly, I had the good
fortune upon arriving at this fair town to meet a
gentleman who will depart on the morrow to join the
Rocky Mountain Fur Company and who may realisti-
cally hope to convey this letter to your hands. I know
that this epistle may take some weeks or months to
reach you; I hope that by then it will still be in a legible
condition. If it is, let me first assure you that by that
time I will have totally recovered from the ordeal I am
about to describe and that my physical appearance will
have returned to normal.
        Several days ago I was making my way to this
town by hired coach to ply my profession on the
dramatic stage and bring some uplifting entertainment
to its citizens. I had prepared an extensive program of
classical - well, no matter, cousin, that's a field that is
alien to you so I will omit the particulars. Suffice it to
say that I was dressed as befits a gentleman of my

station, and would have appeared as choice prey for any party of highwaymen.

We were still a dozen miles from our destination when the coach passed through a narrow and difficult defile. At that moment, we were beset by eight or ten rogues, who swooped down on the carriage, shooting and whooping like demons. My heart leapt, but my driver, a good marksman and hardy teamster, managed to keep them at bay long enough to reach the crest of the rough track and start down the other side. Our jaded horses came to life in the face of danger from the attackers and galloped full throttle. Here the track was too narrow for the brigands to pass us, and they were forced to follow, close behind but scarcely visible in our cloud of dust. Before long however, the madly swaying coach was on the verge of toppling over. The driver, knowing the coach wouldn't last another minute, abandoned ship, choosing what he must have perceived as the lesser of two calamities in dealing with the pursuers. Imagine my chagrin, cousin, when I saw the driver plummet past my window as he leapt for his life! I was abandoned in a careening coffin on wheels that might in the next instant be smashed asunder on the rocks or trees that lined the road. I resolved to follow the driver's example, and grabbing only the articles I had immediately at hand, I dove out the door of the coach.

I rolled over and over upon hitting the ground, but by some miracle I managed to escape serious injury. I lay stunned for a moment at the side of the road and guessed that the pursuers must have galloped past, having missed my escape in the maelstrom of dust. I collected my senses and realized that the coach had indeed crashed fifty yards ahead and the scoundrels were busy rifling the wreckage for anything of value. I took stock of my precarious situation and of the articles I had snatched from the coach as I jumped. I had my new beaver top hat in its leather traveling case and - by great good fortune - my brace of short-barrelled coat pistols and accoutrements.

As you know, cousin, I am less experienced in the ways of the wilderness than you are, and perhaps my judgement was faulty. But I resolved that I would try to slip past the brigands and continue my journey by foot. I had successfully traveled a hundred yards or so, ducking from boulder to tree and escaping detection by the distracted villains, when unfortunately, one of them spotted me and fired his pistol. He missed, and I decided to give him two for one and fired both of my pistols at him. At that, they all scrambled for cover and the siege was on!

My back was to a steep canyon wall and I was protected in front by numerous boulders and trees. I heard voices and saw movement in the whole hundred and eighty degrees of the theatre before me, and I knew I was as surrounded as I could be.

Now I was faced with the necessity of recharging my pistols. I lay out my flask of powder, bullet bag, ramrods, priming horn, and extra flints on the ground before me. In the heat and confusion of unaccustomed combat, my trembling hands made awkward work of reloading. After firing once or twice more, I had dropped everything in such disarray that I could find nothing in the proper order, and could scarcely take my eyes off the position of the enemy to find my accoutrements. It was then, dear cousin Elk, that a stroke of inspiration effaced my mounting panic and made possible my eventual triumph over such oppressive odds!

I concluded that as I handled each component of

every charge, I lost much precious time. I therefore resolved to speed up the loading process in this way: taking out my fine new beaver top-hat and tucking it safely aside, I placed a layer of bullets in the bottom of its carrying case. Over this I emptied my powder flask, covering the bullets to the depth of about an inch. Finally I sprinkled on all my priming powder. This allowed me to reload by merely thrusting the pistols muzzle-first into the hat case. As I pushed the muzzles down to the bottom of the case, the priming powder was forced out the vent into the closed pan, and powder and bullet were squeezed into the bore in the proper order. In this fashion I was able to load and fire at the rate of about eighty shots per minute. You can scarcely imagine the consternation of my assailants, who had never faced such a redoubtable repeater! Their fire was returned more sporadically and seemed to be withering under my voluminous, if not accurate, fusillade. Then my professional training came to my further aid. For it occurred to me that if I were an imposing foe as *one* man with a repeater, what would I be like as *several* men all similarly armed?

In my best theatrical voices, I called to my alleged companions such things as "Say, Thomas, have you got enough ammunition?" and replied in yet another voice, "Yes, Jed, I've got enough to turn back an army." By so projecting and changing my voice, and by dodging from tree to tree, I was able to convince my base enemy that I was really a plurality of defenders. Jubilantly I loaded and fired as quickly as I could, calling out in twenty voices! Forgive my saying so, cousin, but it was the most inspired performance of my career! After a while, the besieged villains sprang for their horses, and I knew that the rout was complete. I was beside myself with joy; though the vanquished would never know that they were defeated by a single man - and a very unaccomplished warrior at that - I was so carried away by my imminent victory that I desired to rub salt into their wounds.

As two or three of the panic-stricken black-guards struggled to mount their dancing and bucking horses, I called out, "Wilson, they're getting away! Prepare to discharge your field piece!" At that time I was redoubling my efforts to load and fire quickly, thrusting first one pistol then the other into the hat box filled with powder and ball. In my attention to the theatrical charade of creating an army of co-defenders, I was distracted from the coordination required to load and fire effectively. To my horror, I bungled and snapped the lock of one pistol as it was thrust into the powder for another load. Naturally, the result was an explosion that shot skyward and singed my hair and beard back to twisted stubble. My jacket was shredded and my face blackened, pocked and blistered. My sight was saved by the spectacles I must continually wear. But my enemy apparently concluded that Wilson had fired our cannon at them, for they sprinted away with nary a backward glance.

By one false move I had kept my victory from being complete and absolute. Yet I had much for which to be thankful. So, gathering up my cherished beaver top-hat - perhaps the product of some of your labors, dear cousin - I proceeded to walk the remaining miles to Boonesborough. I assure you that I cut a most incongruous figure; I arrived in town looking, save for my gleaming new top-hat, as one who had been poorly burned at the stake by savage captors. But I am safe and have been comfortably lodged here for these several days. My wounds have sufficiently healed so that I have been able to carry on my theatrical program, to the gratification of all parties - at least if one is to believe the reviews in the local newspaper. But whatever my success here, cousin, it will take a command performance to better my charade of a few days ago. And for the remainder of my career, I shall never face such a hostile audience as the one for whom I played the intrepid warriors.

That, dear cousin, is the essence of my recent adventure, which will, I trust, compare favorably to some of yours. I hope that this letter finds you well and that you return safely and satisfied with your experiences in the western mountains.

I am, your most obedient servant,
Josiah Hart

A Narrow Escape

I was hunting squirrels last fall and wasn't prepared to meet any large or dangerous game. Imagine my fright upon stepping from the blind side of a great boulder into the dining room of a large black bear sow and two cubs! The great bruin grunted in alarm and pounced for me. I managed to jump backwards at the last instant, and the avalanche of bared fang and claw crashed to earth just a ramrod's length from its intended victim. I dropped my rifle and let fly with my heels, sprinting lickity-clippity through the woods. I knew it was only a matter of yards before the bear caught and devoured me. I could feel her fetid breath on my neck as I spied my only possible salvation: a large hollow log lying on the ground directly in my path. Without breaking stride, I dove headlong into the hollow log and scrambled in as far as I could.

I heard the old sow bellow in frustration at my apparent escape. Momentarily, she began to chew and claw at the end of the log, and she managed to break off a few pieces. By reaching in as far as she could, she raked the soles of my moccasins a couple of times, but couldn't get a purchase on them. Just the same, she scarred them up most beautifully, and as result I'm an easy hoss to track to this day. In her determination to extract me from my refuge, the bear tugged and ripped at the log, finally dislodging it from the depression where it had lain for two decades. Another mighty tug from the sow sent my log and me rolling down a hill. I was gaining speed in my downhill course at an alarming rate when the log broadsided a large boulder, bounced and came to a halt. Dizzy and bruised, I was yet relieved that, despite the impact, my armor had not broken apart to expose me to the avid bear, for she was still intent on having me for dinner. She paced back and forth by my log, growling and gnashing her teeth in frustration.

At long last, the sow decided to relax and outlast me. She sat square on the middle of my hollow log with a *humpf!*, figuring to tackle me with ease as I left by either end.

As I squirmed and sweat bullets, trying to find a trail out of my dilemma, I noticed a ray of sunlight peeping through a hole in the log where a small limb had once branched from the trunk. Alongside that hole, I made out the bear's hind end. Quick as thought I grabbed that bear's tail with two fingers and pulled it through the hole, tying it in a bulky knot on the inside of the log.

I had the advantage of surprise, and the old sow bawled in rage. I knew she was securely fastened to the log, so I scurried out and made to dash away. But my adversary was not to be so easily denied! She took off in hot pursuit, clawing up the forest floor and dragging the log behind her! This time the race was more even, but she was still gaining on me and once again I thought I was a gone beaver.

In a flash of inspiration, I ran between two small oaks growing about six feet apart. I stopped short on the other side, and with a great display of bravado, I turned to face the onrushing mass of ursine rage with my chest thrust out and my hands on my hips. The bear roared again at my gesture of defiance and at the immediate prospect of sating her consuming blood-lust. She cleared the two oaks, but the log she was dragging behind spanned them and instantly checked her charge. Her skin could not contain the forward rush of her bulk; it peeled back from her nose and bared fangs, and three hundred pounds of boned bear meat landed at my feet. I untied the hide from the log and used it as a sack to pack out the meat, leaving the bones

in a heap where they fell. I retrieved my rifle and returned to my camp, well contented with the outcome of
my adventure.

Now, companyeros, I have the only complete,
seamless bearskin you're likely to see, plus a season's
worth of filleted bear meat. What's more, I didn't even
have to dirty my rifle or draw my knife in the course of
the hunt. And if you don't believe this story, come on
over to my cabin; I saved a piece of bark from one of
those oak trees as proof.

Freezing Times

Last year in the moon of the trees popping, my meat supply was getting low and I had no choice but to go after some fresh venison. You'll remember that it was tarnaciously cold and there was an uncommonly deep cover of snow. But because I'm a good horseman and have a fine mount, I didn't hesitate to ride north several miles to where I'd heard that the deer were wintering over. To get there, I had to skirt the settlement; then by sticking to the hills and logging roads I knew pretty well, I calculated I could find some game in a couple hours of riding.

As my trusted cayuse and I headed out of my dooryard, I literally heard the temperature drop to the ground with a crash!, for the mercury had crowded so tight into the ball of my store-bought thermometer that it broke out the bottom and shot into the snow beneath like a pistol bullet. The snow was turning blue from the cold, and as I passed my neighbor, he was putting smudge pots under his cows to thaw them for milking. A short ways beyond his barn, my attention was attracted to a pitiful whimpering. I investigated and found a desperate hound dog frozen fast to a tree by a single thin icicle. He looked mighty eager to get his hind leg back to vertical. He rolled his eyes and swallowed hard as I drew my belt axe and chopped the poor beast free; then he tore away ki-yi-ing down to the cowbarn with nary a backward glance.

A short way out of the settlement, I spotted a flock of ducks frozen in the surface of a pond. I figured I could stroll down and shoot them at leisure; but at my approach, they flapped their wings in unison, pulled the pond out of its banks, and flew away with it. I tried a shot, but the ice was too thick to penetrate it from underneath. So girding myself against the arctic blasts, I headed deeper into the frozen forest.

As I rode along, I bit a chaw of my old twist terbacky to fool my stomach into thinking food was at hand. But the air had turned so cold that my jaws squeaked like a rusty hinge. When I spat, the juice crackled and turned to ice before it reached ground. The snow was so hard we could canter across it without leaving a mark, but the hoofbeats sounded like gunfire and I knew we'd never get close to any game that way. After a few tries, I coaxed Blaze into a sliding diagonal stride in imitation of the Nordic folks who slide over the snow with boards strapped to their feet. That was quick and silent, and soon we were in deer country.

Eventually, I spied a big buck before he saw me. I was shivering so much I had to rest my rifle for the shot. I looked around for a suitable rest, but there was nothing handy. So I exhaled several big puffs of air and stacked the frozen breaths on my saddle horn. Resting my rifle across the top, I fired without even dismounting. Klatch! At first the sparks just fell into the pan with no effect. I looked into the pan, and sure enough, there they lay - a pile of cold, blue sparks. I pinched a few out and warmed them in my mouth. When they were too hot to hold any longer, I spat them into the open pan. The rifle fired and I shot the buck broadside. It was so cold that there was no report. The smoke formed a ten-foot cloud that remained frozen to the muzzle of the rifle. As the bullet found its mark, the deer shattered like glass into a hundred pieces. That at least saved me the trouble of field dressing him. I merely snapped the smoke cloud from my rifle barrel, picked up the pieces of venison, and headed home.

This May, a trapper tending his line in the same area at the time of the first thaw was surprised to hear the report of a rifle and the sound of breaking glass. At the same instant, the snow and leaves and twigs which covered the ground flew about in great agitation, as if blown by a miniature cyclone, though the air was dead calm. When he told me the particulars, I realized it was simply my shot from several months previous breaking out of the deep freeze.

For sure, last winter was a particularly hard one, even for these parts. But the cold wasn't without its positive side, for we had the good sense to open up the root cellar for a while and trap some of that cold air. Then long about July and August when we needed it, we could carry up a bushel basket of it and cool off the cabin. But you know how hot air rises and cold air sinks? Well, even after several months in the root cellar, that cold air still had so much sinking power that it took two men to lift a bushel basket of it!

A Favor Repaid

My quest for turkey and a partridge or two once took me close to a beaver pond not far from here. From a distance, I spied a beaver on the shore that was acting in a very peculiar fashion. As I approached, I discovered that the hapless critter had gnawed through a tree and failed to run clear. The trunk had pivoted on the stump; and, the upper branches being caught in the surrounding tree tops, it had dropped vertically onto the beaver's tail, pinning him in place. The earth was clawed up everywhere within reach, and the unfortunate beaver looked haggard and exhausted from his ordeal. When I first glimpsed him, he was bent double like a hairpin in a fruitless attempt to chew the offending tree trunk from his tail. I judged that he'd been captive for the better part of a day.

The beaver's alarm increased at the sight of a human carrying a fowling piece. For a moment he redoubled his exertion to break free, then seemed to resign himself to fate and become almost apathetic. It's hard to read anything in those beady rodent eyes, but it was clear enough that the poor critter was too spent to defend himself and that all hope of salvation had just abandoned him. I had no interest in dispatching him unless there was no choice - his pelt was far from prime at that season anyway - so I decided to try to free him. I lay down my long fowler and approached him cautiously. He chattered and pulled and stretched his tail to get away from me as I strained to lift the trunk from his rudder. I managed to lift the trunk just enough and his tail slid out from underneath. Once free, he immediately dashed for the shore, but paused for an instant to look back at me before diving out of sight.

Some months later, I went ice fishing at the same place. Unbeknownst to me, the ice was unsafe in certain spots on account of warm springs that gushed to the surface of the pond. I hadn't yet reached the middle of the pond when a patch of rotten ice broke through beneath my feet and I plunged over my head into the frigid water. I lost my senses for an instant, and when I came to, I had drifted from the hole I'd fallen through. Luckily, there were air pockets at certain places under the ice, and I managed to gasp a lung full. In only a few seconds, I was about to succumb to the cold, and I could see the Spirit Trail opening up before me. But just as I was slipping into unconsciousness, I felt a tug on my suspenders and I was aware that an unseen force was pulling me swiftly through the water.

When I came to, everything was dark, save for a few pinholes of light coming in through a wattle roof. I was wet and shivering, but clearly alive. I felt some warmth from two rank, squat forms huddled next to me. At that moment, I realized that I was in a beaver lodge! I reached out and cautiously touched a large animal. His skin crawled and his muscles tensed as I ran my hand down his wet back to his tail, in the middle of which I felt a deep indentation. It was my friend from the previous season's encounter! He had brought me to his diggings, and, with his mate was crowding close enough to revive me with his body heat. He was busy peeling bark from some of his winter's supply of saplings. I suspect he intended to offer me some, but I didn't have much appetite for it. I was pleased to know that my friend had apparently prospered since his close call of some months previous; his pelt was now prime, and he would have weighed a good sixty pounds. I mentally rebuked myself for seeing in my host a mere plew, and was grateful that he couldn't read my thoughts.

After I'd warmed up some and taken stock of my situation, I realized I'd have to secure some vittles. I still had hook, line and bait in my coat pocket and managed to fish through the underwater door of the beaver lodge. In that manner, I was able to sustain myself on survival rations of raw fish for three days. Beaver and mate went about their business and treated me kindly, sharing their warmth and bark strips, which I pretended to accept but secretly cached when they were out for a swim.

For the first day, bright pinholes of light piercing the lodge ceiling told of fair weather outside. The beaver were gone for hours at a time, so I figured they were feeding on shore and working on their dam. During the next morning, the light dimmed and the wind began to whistle around the lodge; an occasional snowflake was carried in on the drafts, and eventually the pinholes disappeared under a blanket of new snow. For the duration of the storm, my hosts stayed close to home, occasionally slipping noiselessly in and out of the water. They were never gone more than ten or fifteen minutes, and as they returned with fresh strips of bark, I realized they were feeding on saplings they had previously cached close to the lodge.

The beaver showed me every consideration. They stood a moment by the doorway upon reentering our living quarters so they could shed some of the excess water from their coats without drenching me. The female regularly groomed her mate by nibbling his fur, and when she turned her attention to my hair, I figured I'd been adopted. I chuckled as I considered that old John Colter had missed this kind of hospitality by not staying long enough in the beaver lodge that sheltered him in his flight from Indian captors many generations ago.

But kind as my hosts were, I knew I had to get free from that confinement and use my limbs again.

Aside from my natural desire to return to my accustomed haunts, I wasn't sure I'd be so welcome as the female came closer to the time she'd give birth to a new litter - and I could tell she already had a good start on that.

At last I felt recovered enough to attempt to leave the beaver's hospitality. The only exit was through the water; I dreaded that prospect, and wasn't sure where to go once I left the lodge. My host must have sensed my intentions, for he indicated by repeatedly shuffling back and forth between my side and the door that I should follow him. I joined him at the door, clutched his tail with both hands, and took a deep breath as he pulled me into the water. Fluttering my feet behind me, I hoped my guide would remember that, unlike him, I couldn't hold my breath for fifteen minutes. Presently we surfaced in a patch of open water where a small stream fed into the pond. As I emerged shivering from the water, I waved to my amphibious friend, who smacked his tail once before ducking below the ice on his return home. Quickly gathering some shredded birch bark and dry twigs, I used my fire kit to kindle a good blaze and dry out. Once thawed, I hiked out to the comfort of hot food and human diggins. Now you know I'll keep my trapline far away from that pond, and if I ever find anyone else's traps up there, I'll spring them and hang them in the trees.

A Rancantankerous Rifle Barrel

I'll tell you the true story of how I spoiled a fine rifle-barrel gun.

I was shooting at a mark with some friends. I was using my favorite match-winner that had a tuned lock, a fine single-set trigger, and a hand-cut, choke-bored, gain-twist barrel. When I stepped up to fire, my friends commenced to hollering and heckling so I'd make a wide shot. I can usually take that kind of treatment; but when they accused me of dry-balling it, I paused and remembered that I truly hadn't poured any powder down the muzzle. So I reached for my ball-puller.

Now I've got a special steel rod with a hardened puller that will cut threads in any ball. Up to that time, I'd never had a chance to try it out. It looked like such a fine rod I allow as how I might have been anxious to use it and show my amigos what a fine piece of equipment I had. So I rammed it down the barrel amidst hoots and guffaws from the other shooters, and sure enough, it bottomed hard. I gave the rod a couple of turns and a good yank, but the rod pulled loose and brought nothing up. I thought that mighty peculiar, so on my next attempt, I leaned on the rod and twisted with all my strength and got a good bite - but then I couldn't budge the rod. So two of my companyeros grabbed the rifle butt and two pulled on the rod, and we had a tug o' war with that rifle that left a trail of sweat and heel marks over two acres of woods and pasture. For all our pulling and twisting and groaning, that rod still wouldn't move.

It was bad enough to have forgotten the powder, but to be bested by a piece of my own equipment was worse! I had to shoot; why, if I was to be defeated in the match, I wanted it to be by the hand of a skilled competitor and not due to the wrath of an inanimate object. So finally I tied my rifle in the crotch of an apple tree and borrowed a farmer's mule. I put a timber hitch around the rod and secured the other end of the rope to the mule's harness and got ready to yank that ball. The mule strained and the apple tree creaked, and it looked like another stalemate. But as I added my strength by pulling on the mule's halter, the rod started to move. I could see we were making progress, so I kept goading the mule on. Suddenly the rod sprang out the muzzle and the mule nearly lunged onto his nose. Success at last!

Well, friends, imagine how quickly my triumph turned to consternation when I untied the rifle from the tree and discovered that I hadn't dry-balled it at all! By Tunket, the rifle was plumb empty, and I'd twisted that ball puller into the face of the breech plug and turned the barrel completely inside-out, like a sock!

But you know, things could have been worse. My inverted barrel has the nicest octagon smooth bore you've ever seen, and I was tempted to use it as is with eight-sided bullets. The only problem was that the sights obstructed the bore. So I took that barrel with the lands and grooves on the outside and used it as a rifling guide for my hand rifling machine. Now I can cut as many barrels as I want; they're as good as the original one, and I'm back in the winner's circle at the rifle matches. That's where I'll stay, too, as long as I stick to doing things right and keep from rabbit-earin' when the competition starts to hecklin'.

Ol' Broken Wind

Harken up, pilgrims, for this be the gospel! I'll tell you about an ol' companyero o' mine who were half painter, half grizz, an' half bull buffler. Yeah, I know that amints to more 'n a hunnert percent, but this coon were some! Now, ol' Broken Wind, as I knowed him, had seen the lizard an' the elephant. Long afore I met him, he'd spent his days larnin' the ways o' all the critters that walks, flies, crawls, or swims. He could hunt and trap as many four-leggeds as he wanted 'cause he understood 'em better 'n even they did. He read sign clearer 'n you hear my words, and I vum he could track a flea across a mile o' cobblestone.

You know, when a normal man flushes a pa'tridge in the timber, oft times he's tarnal lucky jest to catch sight of him again. But ol' Broken Wind would walk straight to the tree where the wing flapper had lighted and blow him out o' the branches without hesitatin'. He claimed he could track the birds through the air and the fishes through the water, the way you and me tracks other critters. Why, I reckon his brain could think so much like a bird's that he could pick out the best trail through the branches.

Broken Wind had powerful medicine in the woods. May my rifle hang fire forever if this ain't true: once he tracked a full-growed bear backwards from where he'd killed it to the place it was born, just for fun. And you know, when most of us follows a track, we're kind of led along real passive-like; if the critter goes through a bramble patch, well, we go through it too; if he takes us through a mucky overgrown swamp, in we plunge. Well, it was different with Broken Wind. He was so savvy he could follow several tracks at one time; and by second-guessin' where his quarry would be laid up watchin' for him, he could force the four-legged in any direction he wanted. Sometimes he'd deliberately make noise or throw a rock or take a shortcut and surprise the critter, who'd bound off in the opposite direction, just where Broken Wind wanted him. That's a technique he called *drive-trackin'*, and he's th' only hunter I ever seen who could do it. Most often he'd use it to drive the critter close to his cabin before shootin' 'im so's he wouldn't have to drag the carcass so far. You see, when you get as good as him, it can be a problem to haul back all the game from a day's hunt. I'll show you what I mean.

One day he was out followin' a good deer track. He knew the lay of the land and figured the buck would have to follow the terrain to a crossin' at the falls where the river gets shallow. Comin' through the timber, he unseated a pa'tridge that took off in a different direction from the deer trail he was followin', so he decided to do a little experiment. By jumpin' that bird several times and changin' its direction, he was able to keep it headed along the deer track. Before long, he came to the falls, and what does he see but his buck preparin' to cross the river. His pa'tridge were in a tree on th' other side, and the falls was hoppin' with salmon headin' upstream to spawn. He lay down on his belly to get the right line o' fire, and at exactly the right instant, he touched off the shot, which passed through the buck and caught a big salmon just behind the gills as it made a leap to clear the falls. Of course the bullet sailed straight to the pa'tridge and knocked her right out o' the tree. The pa'tridge fell down like a stone onto the back of a rabbit who died from fright. I later congratulated Broken Wind on the shot, but he was a little disappointed with it. "Heck, I guess I unthoughtedly rushed the shot; it weren't till I pulled the trigger that I noticed the tom turkey in the clearin' beyond the falls. If I'd 'a only seen 'im..."

But that's just the way Broken Wind was. Why, he had so many inborn woods skills and such speed and endurance that he weren't satisfied with exploits that would do most of us proud. I'll give you an idea of how quick this man were. Once he were drivin' along with a wagon-load of Hazard's superfine gun powder to deliver to the rendezvous. The sky clouded up, and along come the rain and thunder and lightning, and a big bolt struck a keg of powder. It wasn't more than a bushel-basketful of powder that had burned up before Broken Wind could stamp the fire out. But you know, there was one time when he were too quick for his own good. He'd shot at a turkey on the ground and ran up to it so fast that his own shot hit him in the hindside, and the gobbler flew away unharmed.

Now ol' Broken Wind were in league with a fox for a time. He'd found the critter as a pup and studied him so carefully as he brought him up that he understood every twitch of ear and whisker, and he could actually *communicate* with him. Not word for word, of course, but ideas and facts directly. Now what most folks don't savvy is that all the other critters can do the same as Broken Wind and his accomplice. Rabbits can communicate with squirrels, squirrels with chipmunks, and so forth all the way down the ladder. Well, friends, this fox had access to information straight from the frogs, the worms, the skeeters, the porkypines, and other four-leggeds (although not all the critters was on direct speakin' terms with him, on account of his eatin' habits). So Broken Wind had a channel of information from all the animals and could learn the approachin' weather from the migratin' wing-flappers, the location of fishin' worms, and where the deer was yarded up. In exchange for this information, he shared bones and trimmin's from his bounty with brother Reynard the fox, who commenced to grow plump and lazy since he didn't have to hunt no more.

The partnership lasted till the other critters figured out how they was betrayed. Then they ganged up on Reynard and cooked his goose. When the porky-pines got done wrasslin' with him, he had as many quills as hairs, but they were all pointin' the wrong way. The skunks of the forest stood in line to do their best head-stand in front of that sorry four-legged cactus, and every woodcock passin' through fired a volley of spatter on him. They abandoned that fox for dead, and not one flesh-eater of the woods had appetite to chaw on his carcass. But after a day he came to, and Reynard, broken and half blind, and forever exiled from the animal kingdom, limped back to Broken Wind's diggin's.

He was foamin' at the chops, and deprived of his usual sense and caution. He had the bad luck to blunder up to Broken Wind when he was takin' a snooze on the porch. And as the hunter woke up to that vision, he thought he was bein' attacked by a lucivee, so quick as lightnin' he grabbed his fusil and shot the fox between the eyes. That mistake was a turnin' point in Broken Wind's fortune for it seems he couldn't get over the demise of the fox.

Little by little, without the help of his four-legged partner, Broken Wind seemed to lose his prowess. His mind would wander from the hunt, and he couldn't read sign. His former stealth gave way to a clumsy ramshacking through the woods so that most critters heard him a half mile away. He seldom got a chance to shoot, but when he did, a bad flinch sent the ball wide of the mark. After a while, a discouraged and hungry Broken Wind found himself wondering if he'd have to leave the woods.

It took one more stroke of bad luck to persuade Broken Wind to forsake his woods ways and take up a safer occupation as stable hand in the settlements. You know, he had become so familiar with his long-arm that he was guilty of a couple of sins against safe gun handling. Oft times he blew down the barrel between shots, and he'd spit bullets down on top of his powder charge instead of pushin' them down with his loading stick. I swan, that takes some powerful wind when you're shootin' a tight-patched ball from a rifled-barrel gun. Now one time in the season when the leaves puts on their warpaint, he'd dry-balled his gun just when he needed a shot at a fine buck. He couldn't find his bullet-puller so he figgered that if he could use his breath to load his barrel, he could use it to *unload* it as well. He started to suck on the muzzle of his rifle, but the barrel was fouled from a couple of shots and the bullet wouldn't budge. So he used all the strength in his leathery bellows and sucked as hard as he could. I was afraid his head would cave in, but instead, when the bullet finally broke loose, it shot up the barrel as if it had a full charge of powder behind it. It caught Broken Wind unawares, and he scarcely was able to duck out of the way in time. The bullet creased his head right above his ear. Since that time, he's worked at the livery stable, and he's doing right fine. Seems like he gets along with the horses like nobody else - almost like he and the horses can communicate with each other, I heard the owner say.

Them's the facts, companyeros. By Tunket, all this jaw-flappin' gives a body a ramdacious hollow in the meat bag. Pass me that platter so I can goozle up some of them fine boudins!

Delivered From The Spirit Trail

Some skeptics and pork-eaters may doubt the truth of this tale, but I swear by my Green River that these are the unvarnished facts.

Several seasons back I was skulking through the brush after fresh venison when the tracks I was following took me on a slew of double backs and figure-eights. The crafty white-tail must have caught my scent, for he led me through the most toilsome terrain in these hills. I clambered on all fours through the evergreens, skidding down several slopes only to scramble up the same grade a few hundred yards beyond. Why, some of those ravines were so narrow I could stand at the bottom and touch both sides with my outstretched arms. You know the visibility and the tracking were mighty poor under those conditions, and after a couple hours without so much as a glimpse of the quarry, I was beginning to wonder if I was still on the right set of tracks. The sun was already sinking when I realized that all familiar landmarks had been swallowed up in my twisted back trail. I had no wish to back track through that miserable terrain anyway, and resolved to find an easier path out.

As I crested the next rise, I entered yet another piece of rugged country jammed with massive boulders, shallow caves, blueberry bushes and blackberry tangles. It looked like the last place the glacier had stopped before heading back north to get more rocks. Claw scarred tree trunks, upturned logs, and large piles of scat indicated clearly that this was prime bear territory. Human intrusion wasn't likely to be appreciated, so I checked the priming on my .54 just in case I met one of the rightful tenants of this property.

I was clearly miles from camp, and in the failing light, I paused to consider whether to spend the night there or attempt to find my way in the dark. As I scanned my surroundings, I sensed that somewhere close by in the deep shadows, a pair of eyes kept watch on me from beneath heavy antlers. Shooting light was already gone so I gave up the pursuit and decided to try to get my bearings by climbing a derelict oak a few hundred yards away. The tree had lost its top decades ago, but from its highest point, I would have a view of the surrounding forest and a chance to recognize some distant landmark. The oak was about six feet across at the base and four feet broad at the break. The ground nearby and trunk had been worked by all manner of woods dwellers, from woodpeckers to porcupines to bears.

I leaned Ol' Thunderclap against the opposite side of the tree and clambered to the top. From that vantage point, I discovered a familiar ridge line I'd often used as a landmark, but it was miles to the east, and I concluded that it'd be wiser to stay put for the night. I also discovered that the oak was hollow for farther down than I could see.

The sun rested momentarily behind the hilltops before pulling its last rays over the brow with it. I decided to linger and enjoy the sunset from my perch and take a few draws of kinnick-kinnick through my clay bowl. I sat on the edge of the trunk and dangled my feet into the hollow center, enjoying the fresh-scented breeze and contemplating the pleasant night of camping in store for me. I felt no haste to gather firewood, for the ground was strewn all about with seasoned branches shed over time by my rude throne.

My mood was shattered when, as I shifted my weight a little, the wood under my seat broke loose and I pitched moccasins-first into the bowels of that hollow tree! I fell a good ten or twelve feet before becoming jammed into a tight spot. The sudden crunch knocked the wind out of me and I saw my first set of stars that night.   Dust and rotten wood rained down on my upturned face for two minutes and nearly suffocated me.

My arms were stretched full length overhead and there was no room to move arms or legs to climb out. My possibles bag and powder horn were jammed up tight under my chin, and I gazed straight out the top of that hollow oak. Worst of all, my pipe was still lit, just inches from the spout of my powder horn. I could only hope that the stopper was still in place, for I had visions of my head being shot out of that tree like an iron ball from a cannon barrel.

As I gazed straight out the top of the oak, I watched the sky turn from red to grey to black. A few stars were visible. Now that view wasn't exactly disagreeable, but to this pilgrim's way of thinking, there just wasn't enough of it to enjoy properly. Believe me, this child was mighty desperate to get free.

It was nigh impossible to breathe. The air in the tree was thick and damp; I had splinters and itches where I couldn't reach, and my arms ached from being stretched overhead. The only things I could move were my fingers, which I repeatedly clenched and released to relieve the tingling in my hands.

Several hours later, I was no closer to escaping from that tree, and I had just about decided I was going to go under right there. An oak casket didn't seem too unworthy of this old stump-jumper, but I'd always pictured it a little different - horizontal, at least, and a little more comfortable. My friends and relations would never learn what had become of me, and some chance hunter in a distant decade would marvel at a skeleton encased in the decaying remains of a fallen tree.

My gloom was interrupted when, all of a sudden,

I felt a commotion on the outside of the trunk and heard a hellacious clawing and raking. In an instant, all the stars were blotted out as a great black bear backed down the hollow tree in another shower of dust and splinters! Momentarily soft bear parts settled onto my upstretched hands, and I clamped on as hard as I could with the only part of my body I could move. The old boar hooted and scrambled up the hollow tree like he'd been fired from a mortar, pulling me right behind! Now the tree was a powerful tight squeeze for me, but the bruin eased my passage with a generous coating of lubricant. When we got to the top, I released my hold, and he jumped headlong through the branches, breaking several on the way to the ground. He knocked over my rifle, which discharged harmlessly but compounded his fright. He crashed off through the woods, never looking back, and I could hear him bawling as he ran over the next ridge.

A short while later, the sun was up and I hiked back to my camp. I spent hours pulling splinters from unaccustomed places like my eyebrows and armpits. Then I threw away my handmade buckskins and soaked my battered and fetid body in a hot bath of lye soap to draw out the aches and the stench.

That, my friends, is how I became one of the onliest people around who can claim the questionable distinction of having clutched a live bear by the delicate parts and lived to tell the tale. And you know, I've met hunters who have been to those parts since then. They tell of seeing what they take to be an albino bear that's so wary of humans that they never get more than a ghost-like glimpse; me, I think it's my old friend Sam - short for Samaritan, as I've dubbed him - who merely lost the color in his pelt on account of the fright I gave him. I've never been back to that spot to hunt bear, for

I owe that bruin a debt of gratitude for pulling me out of a tight spot and saving my hair.

The Great Buffler Chase

Come all you old buckskinners and listen to my song,
And please do not grow weary, I'll not detain you long,
Concerning some wild cowboys who did agree to go,
And spend a Summer pleasant on the range of the
buffalo.
-The Buffalo Skinners-

Alright, boys, since you've asked me and won't take no for an answer, I'll tell you about my great chase after the pte-wakan, the medicine buffalo. You see, to begin with, it was my fortune to rescue a young Brule chief from the Spirit Trail. Sakehanska, or Long Claws by name, lay in a heap on the trail at the foot of a cliff where he had tumbled, weak from fasting through a long vision quest. His leg looked to have another joint in it between the hip and the knee, so I gave a good yank to set it straight and bound it in a makeshift splint. The brave was pretty well played out when I found him, but he jerked awake when I tugged on his leg - and I swan you would have too, by Tunket! He didn't seem alarmed at being helpless in the hands of a dog face - I suppose he was just too weak to resist. I succeeded in getting him to take a little wasna, or pemmican, and some water from my canteen.

I dragged him on a travois behind my pack horse and brought him to his village. When we drew near, I was afraid that people might think the chief was dead and that I was the villain, but I figured I could count on Sakehanska to stick up for me. At our approach, a sentinel signaled an alarm and the hackles on my neck stood at attention as a handful of mounted braves dashed out of the village with blood in their eyes. I clutched my belt pistol nervously, but as I turned in the saddle I saw Sakehanska signing the urgent message he could not shout above the din of the charging horsebacks. In that crucial instant, my life hung in the balance, and the picture of the gesticulating chief is graven in my memory: with exaggerated motions, he drew an index finger across his forehead, held aloft an index and middle finger, then made short chopping motions with both open hands. The right index laid along his open left palm and a thumb jerked at his own chest completed the message which said that the white friend had helped him, and I was allowed to keep my hair.

The howling braves raced in circles around us and fired their trade muskets into the air as a welcome to the chief. As they escorted us into the village, a crowd turned out to meet us, and I was relieved to see that they were smiling.

My visit to the village would make another story, boys, but let me just say that the chief was mighty grateful for my help. Indian hospitality can be real fine, and there's nobody more generous when you're on their good side. If'n you do right by 'em, you might know that first-hand some day. But you know, I was glad he didn't have an eligible daughter, for I didn't need any extra baggage on my journey.

I was headed out to rendezvous with some companyeros to plan a trip to the Shinin' Mountains for some trappin', so I had a *schedule* to stick to and I was mighty anxious to get under way. Before I left, though, Sakehanska insisted on presenting me with a new blanket gun and his fastest horse - both of which I could use, and which I accepted with true gratitude. Horse and gun, he assured me, were endowed with the strongest medicine. The crowd hollered as we shook hands, and we parted as friends.

I left the village and pulled foot toward the southwest. I knew it was merely a matter of time before

I had a chance to put my new gifts to the test.

Three days out from the village, I was just stirring in my robes at first light. My camp was by a lazy stretch of the Flatwater River, and my Witney blanket was pulled up over my face to keep the skeeters at bay. In my half-sleep, I heard what I first thought was thunder, then an earthquake. But then I jerked awake and bolted out of my robes - dashing to the top of the nearest rise, I saw 'em comin': a dust cloud about a half-mile off told of a herd of bufflers bearin' down on my camp with a full head o' steam. I figgered they was goin' to make for the river, so I took that as a sign to skedaddle. I pulled the picket on my horse, shouldered my possibles and bedroll, and grabbed a handful of jerky and hardtack to eat as I rode.

My pony and I cut dirt toward the south to get clear of the main part of the herd. My dry breakfast reminded me of how good some fresh buffler would set in my meat bag, so I headed Petala - my new mount - into the mass of critters. I could feel him tense with excitement, and I knew he'd done this many times. Old Sakehanska had trained this one well.

Now boys, remember that this was August. Things was parched and brown everywhere. It was barely daylight, and you could already feel the heat buildin' up. The dust was fine as flour, and it penetrated into the bottom o' your lungs; the sweat ran like black streams on man and horse before the chase even began. I renewed the priming on the blanket gun and cached a couple of spare balls in my mouth.

Honest, boys, I never straddled an animal as fast as Petala! You know, his name means "Little Fire," and I swan he took off so fast he must have had fire in his blood. He charged into them buffler like he had a jalapeño under his tail, with never a care for danger from beast or prairie. He could turn on a half-dime, and his speed fairly scared me, boys. When we dived into the crowd, some of the bufflers veered away and the herd started to change direction. I picked out a fat cow and gave chase. We were on her in a minute. Amid the thundering hooves, I didn't expect to hear the shot; and you know, I had all I could do to see the target through the dust. But when we pulled alongside and I made to shoot, the cow somersaulted headlong over a smaller buff that had stepped into her way. I saw the spinning form skid over the prairie in front of us like a tumble-weed with a dozen legs cutting through the maelstrom of dust. I thought we were goners, but Petala stretched his neck out and bounded over that buffler like it weren't nothin' and landed twenty feet beyond, still goin' at a full gallop.

There was no turnin' back now, so we plunged through the surging bufflers. I felt a mite weak in the knees after our near collision, I tell ye, but ol' Petala was just gettin' warmed up. Then at the same instant we both spotted her: the biggest cow you could imagine, and so dark she was almost black; Petala whinnied loud as away we flew to catch her. I struggled for breath and wiped my eyes in the swirling dust, but Petala seemed unaffected. The cow was wise to us, and she tried every trick to give us the slip. Several times she gained some distance by stickin' us in clusters o' slower critters as she galloped on. But gradually we forced her to the edge of the herd, where we pulled up alongside.

I reached over to put the muzzle of the blanket gun behind her shoulder and yanked on the trigger: KLATCH-POOF! That put my spleen in an uproar, for by puttin' my life on the line, I'd paid for a heart shot and got only a flash in the pan! I snum I could 'a' won a cussin' contest then and there, and maybe set some records; for I could hear my voice over the thundering hoof-beats, and I never repeated myself in the minute it cost me to grab my horn and reprime. A second time my firelock only flashed, and I realized I hadn't loaded it before mounting up. Petala grunted and broke wind as if to say, "You incompetent!" But he was right, boys, for I'd gone in to fight them bufflers with an empty gun.

If you've never tried to reload at a full gallop, you can't appreciate what I went through to get a charge into that barrel. I spilled a couple drams o' precious powder before I finally got enough down the muzzle to carry the ball. I chipped a tooth as I spat one bullet down the bore, and I thumped the butt on my thigh to settle the charge.

Well, companyeros, that cow struck off to the west, leavin' the whole herd behind, and we lit out lickity-clippity in pursuit. Petala showed his mettle; he dug in like a tick and I knew we would not be denied victory.

But I never saw anything like it, friends; that critter still managed to stay ahead of us! Every time we drew closer, the she-buffler would shovel on some more coal and open up the lead again.

The contest soon became one of horse and buffler, and I was little more than a spectator. I snum that cow had strong medicine; I began to fear that she was a true pte-wakan, an unhuntable *creation* buffler. But Petala galloped on.

We were now on a beeline toward the west. The sun was high, and the heat intense. Sweat poured from Petala, and my tongue started to swell. Fortunately, we had to swim a couple of broad rivers. That gave us some refreshment, but the quarry maintained her lead in the water as well as on land. I felt a mite uneasy, for I had no idea where our chase would take us or how long we'd be gone. I was afraid my mount would drop from the exertion and heat and leave me stranded; but boys, little did I yet know of his determination and strength! I tried to rein him in, but he would have none of it. So I charged on, a prisoner on my own horse.

Near sundown I spied a bright glow on the prairie before us at a mile's distance. My horse tailed the buffler like a shadow, but we still couldn't close for a shot with the short-barreled trade gun. Presently I identified the glow as a campfire. The buffler led us straight through the camp, scattering embers, firewood, pots and gear in all directions. Men jumped for their lives! As we sped through, I recognized my companyeros and hallooed a frantic greeting. In my last glimpse of them, every man-jack one of 'em stood like slack-jawed sleepwalkers, gawkin' in disbelief at the shambles of their camp.

Well, boys, on we sped through the night and entered the foothills of the Stony Mountains around midnight. Before long, I slumped forward on my mount's neck, plum played out from hunger and the day's hardships. I awoke several times in the next hours as we scrambled over rocks and up the mountainsides. First marmots, then mule deer, then elk, then bighorn sheep clambered out of our way in panic as we sped through their haunts.

Many times we had to duck and dodge as stones flew from the buffler's hooves and hummed past our ears like rifle shots. In one of my moments of wakefulness, violent snow squalls assailed us, and on both sides of us, tree tops and branches snapped off in the gale. Both animals often dislodged rocks, sometimes sliding backwards with them, but always checking their fall at the last moment. I saw rocks plummet into endless, black chasms at every hand, while up above, wild clouds pursued each other across the face of an indifferent moon.

But the clouds' chase was no more chilling, no more unearthly than the one I was caught up in, boys; I found myself wonderin' if I was chasin' the Devil or ridin' him! The clattering of hooves on rock soon became muffled with snow, and the animals sometimes wallowed and bounded like sea-porpoises to get through.

At last, I couldn't bear to witness the passages we galloped through at such breakneck speed, so I clenched my eyes shut and clutched Petala's mane. I shivered throughout the night, only partly on account of the cold and wind. I believe, boys, I used some of the same words I'd uttered on the prairie earlier in the day, but in a different spirit!

The sun was already high when I next awoke and found that the terrain, no longer devoid of vegetation, was leveling out under our feet. We had galloped completely across the Rockies and were now heading into the *desert*! The heat was again unbearable, and I mingled my sweat with Petala's. I sensed that this chase had to end soon or we'd run ourselves into the next world.

My head spun in the shimmering heat and played tricks on me. At times I thought I saw *two* buffs and I feared Petala was chasin' the wrong one! I called to him and reined hard and about wore out my quirt tryin' to get him to respond. But he was transfixed, and as it turned out, he was right, boys. For at last the buffler seemed to slow visibly and she looked over her shoulder, alarm in her eyes. Petala sensed that victory was at hand and surged ahead with renewed persistence as I checked my priming.

At that moment our shadows hung right beneath us. The blanket gun was so hot under the desert sun that I could scarcely touch it, and I was afraid the shot might cook off before I was ready to pull the trigger. We closed to within twenty feet of the buffalo - not quite near enough for a shot - when what to my *great astonishment* do I see, boys, but a ramdacious jet of steam shoot spontaneously out o' that buffler's hide with an ear-splittin' hiss! Down she goes, rollin' over and over with high-pressure steam shootin' out in twenty directions like a locomotive made from a colander. A jet of steam scalded my leg as we galloped past, and I was so flummuxed I swallowed one o' my spare bullets.

Old Petala either didn't believe his eyes, or was too mesmerized by the chase to see that his quarry lay motionless on the desert floor twenty rods behind, and I couldn't get him to haul about. Finally I thought to try to bring him around by firing my shot. That seemed to break the trance, and we returned to examine the medicine buffalo that had led us through the most *incredible* - yes, I see it in your eyes, boys - chase you'll ever see. That buffalo's medicine was so powerful, friends, I half expected to find she had a forked tail; but the truth was even stranger, and I hope to be shot if this ain't true.

For imagine my astonishment on examining the buffalo: she lay in a formless heap - no shape at all, boys, like she was pure liquid inside her skin, sloshin' back and forth like ocean waves; and steam was still hissin' out o' her hide. Close examination revealed the truth: she'd run so hard and hot under the desert sun that she'd *pressure-cooked* into a self-contained bag of buffalo stew! When she brushed a barrel cactus on the charge across the desert, she poked a pinhole in her hide, and that took so much steam out of her that down she went. I gorged on boudins and broth, and even my mount partook. And he'd earned it, boys! My horse is the only living witness to the whole of this adventure, but it's true, every bit. Why, just see if he denies a word of it!

Well, it took us three days to retrace our steps to my companyeros. I now had plenty of confidence in my new horse, but my musket was unproven. That was to come the next day, when, as we entered a narrow draw, there come a whole cavvyard of starved and menacin' ... But you're right, boys, that's another tale, and I see you're yawnin' and hankerin' for the robes; let's save that one for another time.

How I Saved My Life By Shooting Myself

Mind you, hear me out to the end of this tale! Nobody jumps out of the wagon mid-stream or you'll miss my drift.

I ain't always been so shriveled and crotchety, but I have been uncommonly thin all my days. When I was young, I was downright skinny, and there wadn't a thing I could do about it. I was so active that meat just wouldn't stick to me.

One day in early fall - I s'pose I was about twenty at the time - I'd finished all the barnyard chores early and got a little ahead by orderin' a wagon load o' hay from Pelatiah McCutcheon at his place, about a half-mile up the lane from our'n. Ol' Pelatiah was a hard-workin', honest sort who never said much. You could always take him at his word, and when he said he'd be by with the hay at four o' clock the day after tomorrow, I knew I could count on it.

So I grabbed my gun and went out a-huntin' far into the North Andiron Bog to see if I could find a big deer. You know, in them days I used to run the deer down just like old Ethan Allen did, leastwise accordin' to legend. I'd pick up the track I wanted to follow and sort of dog trot along real quiet until I saw the deer, and then the chase was on! A deer's a pretty fair runner in a sprint, but you see, I was a lean long-distance runner and could outlast most any four-legged. Heck, I'd cover miles in a day runnin' down a deer. Well, that partick-lar day I was on a good track an' wadn't payin' too close attention to where I was steppin' 'cause I was tryin' to spy the deer through the thicket. All of a sudden I come up with a jerk and got my ankle all squinched up hard in a hemlock root and sprained it near off. I snum that was a fine way to spile the hunt! I'd lost a fine load o' venison, but even worse, I was stranded a couple o' miles from the nearest settlement. My leg hurt so bad

I couldn't hop nor hobble nor drag it.

I could hear runnin' water not far off, so I managed to belly-crawl over to this little stream. That wadn't more'n a hunnerd yard, but it was just enough to convince me 'at I had no hope o' draggin' myself out o' there. I let my hurt leg trail in the cold stream, and even though the movement o' the water made it ramdacious sore, the water kept the swellin' from goin' above my knee. I sat for a long time wishin' I'd been more keerful and wonderin' how I was goin' to get out o' that pickle.

I had my seventy-five caliber smooth-bore with me - an ol' parts-barrel Brown Bess it were, that had survived Rogers' retreat from St. Francis, or so my grandad tol' me - and I fired several shots with that to try to attract some attention. I hollered at the top o' my bellows, whistled on an acorn cap till I was near deaf, and built a smoky fire. But it was all for naught. I could 'a' whistled and yelled till doomsday without bein' found, and for the first time in my life I was gettin' scared o' goin' under.

As it turned out, I was stranded there for two days with no food or hope of bein' discovered. My leg was worse instead o' better, and I was gettin' weak from lack o' food. Oh, I chewed my mockersons like some o' the old timers did, but that was mighty poor fare. I even managed to improve it a little with the help of my old Brown Bess. You see, when it was restocked some years ago, ol' Varney, the gunsmith up to the settlements, used a good piece o' native sugar maple. Heck, I could still see the marks in the stock where the spiles had been stuck into the wood in the Springtime. So anyway, I bored a hole or two into the stock with the point o' my Green River an' managed to suck out just enough maple sap to flavor the leather o' my mockersons. And all the time I was stuck there, d' you think a squirrel or pa'tridge 'd come into range? Heck, I could 'a' been in the town square for all the game movin' through that part o' the woods. Now remember I was so young an' skinny that I had no leeway in the face o' starvation, and it took a quick toll on my spare frame. My head was playin' tricks on me; I imagined the hills to be mounds o' potatoes and the trees to be stalks o' corn, and cold switchel runnin' in the creek. But I still had enough sense to know that I'd have to set my thinkin' machine to work if I was goin' to save my skin.

Now as I said, I was naturally slight; but after two days of fasting, I was jeroosly skinny, not much bigger 'round than a garter snake. During my first night out, the coyotes came prowlin' around just out o' sight to keep watch on me, thinkin' to have an easy meal. But on the second night, they decided I wasn't worth the wait and slunk off to find better eats than this poor bull. You know, during the day when the sun beat down on me, I'd just stick my ramrod into the ground and rest in its shade. And that's what gave me the idea I needed.

I checked the flint in my Brown Bess and double-charged the piece. Then I cut the cuffs off my union suit and stuffed 'em down the barrel as waddin'. I used one o' the thongs from my mockersons to tie the musket to my wrist. Sightin' homeward - high and south by southwest - I leaned the musket against a blow-down, primed it, and set it on full cock.

Then I took my patch grease and smeared it all over me starting at the soles of my feet. I squeezed feet first into the muzzle of the musket, keeping my greased shirt close about me, and I learned first-hand what a patched rifle ball feels like as it starts down the barrel. With lots of squirming, I got myself firmly seated against the powder charge with my body from the armpits upward sticking out the muzzle.

I checked my time piece and saw that it was quarter to four in the afternoon - exactly what I wanted. So I checked the line of sight once again and reached down to push on the trigger with a forked stick. Scratch-kerboom! Out the muzzle I flew and over the treetops toward Farmer McCutcheon's field. When I took off, the thong jerked the musket around and away it came with me. You know, when I sailed out the muzzle, my head spun enough as it were; I'm glad I had a smoothbore instead of a rifled-barrel gun!

I was thinkin' it was a pity the musket wadn't loaded again, for as I sailed along I could see I was gainin' on some geese that were headed south to their winterin' ground. But I didn't need another shot anyway, 'cause I caught up with 'em and two of 'em died o' fright when I flew through the back o' their V. I managed to catch both of 'em as they started to drop.

As I sailed over a familiar rise, I spied McCutcheon's field and knew that Bess had shot true again. The barn grew bigger and bigger as on I flew, and I almost got caught on McCutcheon's weathervane; but I merely brushed it and set it to spinnin' like a target in a shootin' gallery. In the next instant, I landed plop! in Pelatiah's wagon as he was headin' out his gate to deliver the hay to my barnyard. We pulled into my dooryard at exactly four o' clock, just as I knew we would. Pelatiah didn't ask questions, but I felt a little awkward, just droppin' in on him like that, all cata-wampus from my ordeal; so handing him one goose, I simply said I'd had some luck huntin' and that he could have Hilda cook that one up and I'd tell him the story later. That night I ate a whole goose; and with enough vittles and good rest my leg was soon strong enough to walk on.

It's a good thing I never lived so high that I had too much saddle girth to squeeze into that barrel o' mine! 'Cause that's how I ended up savin' myself by shootin' myself. I swan that's a leetle diff'rent from what you was thinkin' when I started this tale now isn't it!

THE CATAMOUNT AND
THE BIG SWALLOW

My cousin Gid Whitlock enjoys being known as Sidehill County's most accomplished - and reckless - hunter and yarn-spinner. He secured his reputation as a ring-tail roarer when, several years back, he was contracted by the municipal zoo down at Three Forks to supply a pair of bobcats. He strode into town one morning carrying a pair of live animals, one clamped tightly under each arm. They clawed and hollered like a dozen devils, but Gid just grinned and gloated in his notoriety.   He walked unannounced into the zoo director's office, shut the door behind him, and turned the cats loose. That made him a local celebrity overnight. But it didn't necessarily win him the admiration of the masses, for you see, he is also recognized as the county's most unwashed human being. He lives alone in a tiny cabin and seldom mixes with other people, so he doesn't feel obliged to wash. Besides, if there's one thing Gid hates, it's bathing in cold water. He spends so much time hunting and tracking that he's always behind in putting his firewood by, and he considers it wasteful to burn his scant and hard-gotten firewood to heat water for washing. I usually visit him in the Spring or the Fall when he can keep his cabin windows open.

This will give you an idea of how much of a stranger he is to soap. Last summer, he went to a local rifle match where they had an egg shoot. You know how that works: the contestants fire at raw eggs swinging on a string in the breeze; the ones who miss have to eat their eggs, and the ones who hit get lots of laughs. Well, Gid and a couple of others had missed their targets, which had been hanging in the sun for a couple of hours. One by one the shooters reluctantly cracked their eggs open and choked them down. You never saw such a gallery of whiskey-faces! Gid was the last. He let on like he just couldn't stomach it; he hesitated and tried to beg off, but of course there was no escape from swallowing that egg. The more he protested, the keener the spectators' interest grew, and folks crowded in close to savor Gid's discomfort when he finally swallowed the bitter pill of defeat. At the last instant, he got a gleam in his eye and chomped into that egg, shell and all, just as if he were eating an apple! Yolk splattered all over his beard as Gid munched with gusto. People hollered in disbelief and revulsion, and if there had been any citified ladies present they would have fainted at the spectacle of Gid's gaping mouth crunching away like a dog with a chicken bone. At the end, he licked all his fingers and laughed out loud at the spectacle he had created at the others' expense. Some speculated that he had intentionally missed his target just for the chance to nettle his comrades. The point is, though, that folks who later bumped into him, when the last leaves were dropping off the trees, noticed that he still had eggshells glued in his crusty beard.

I guess I'm the closest thing to a friend Gid has, and I've been able to speak frankly with him about his personal habits. Last Fall we were hunting near Spectre Pond. In the morning as we dressed, I saw Gid remove his stiff and grimy socks and replace them forthwith on the opposite feet. To my query, he answered indignantly, "What in Tunket does it *look* like I'm doin'? I'm *changin' my socks*, you durn fool!" He defended his practice by saying, "Tell me, ol' hoss, how many times you change your socks in a month."

"Why, I change them every day, of course!"

"Then lay off o' me! I ain't the one that's got the problem if every month you dirty sixty socks to my two!" He was a hard man to argue with, and I had to admit that there were no flies on him - in a figurative sense, of course.

I changed my approach, hoping to strike the mark with a line of reasoning which he might grasp readily. "You know, Gid, I'd think you'd try to get rid of as much human scent as possible before heading after game; the critters are likely to smell you coming." He countered that if he were to wash, he'd only smell human again, and the game would scent him a mile off and skedaddle. "At least this way," he countered, "they don't take me for a hunter. Why, it's taken me months to build up my cover, and I'd hate to ruin it in jest seven or eight washings. Besides, ever notice hows many critters is *attracted* to the smell o' carrion?" I finally despaired of changing his ways; in any case Gid soon put the subject to rest for good.

Last week I went to visit Gid at his cabin around dinner time. His cabin is a sight, and I always marvel at the number of antlers, skulls and stretched pelts that cover its walls - the fruits of his hunting and trapping. Gid's hard to find during the day - and at night when he's hunting 'coons - but you can always count on his being home for the evening meal. To my surprise, he was nowhere to be found. His rifle was gone from the hooks by the chimney, so I knew he was out hunting. I returned at breakfast the next day, and still no sign of Gid. That was very uncharacteristic, and I became concerned that some mishap had befallen him. I had my own chores to do during that day, but returned to Gid's clearing at dinner time to see if he had appeared. The cabin was still empty. I intended for a moment to leave him a note to contact me when he returned, but thought better of it; there were no writing implements in his diggin's, he couldn't read a note anyway, and he'd only wonder what kind of national calamity had required that someone put a written message on his door.

I hung around Gid's place until dusk, and was about to give up waiting for him when he plodded out of the woods and across the clearing. He appeared haggard and disheveled, and his hair was plastered in wild tangles against his head. He carried what appeared to be a large sack over one shoulder, and a huge slab of meat under the opposite arm. "Howdy, Ol' Hoss! What brings you here?" he grinned. Gid's teeth always reminded me of the dilapidated fence around Widow Gorton's place; pickets leaned toward all points on the compass, and in two or three places, it looked like the gate had been left open.

"I was concerned when you didn't come back for supper last night."

"Why, it's mighty neighborly of you to look after me. But you ought to know better than to worry. Come on in; we'll scramble up some grub in no time."

With a sigh he dumped his shapeless burden into the shadows beside his cabin and trudged inside. He lit a lamp and struck flint to steel to kindle a fire in the venerable iron cook stove. Gid tossed on a last stick of wood and clanked the rusty lid into place to contain the billowing smoke. The fire was visible through several cracks in the stove walls, and from time to time a fragrant plume of smoke escaped into the tiny room. Soon he was frying up some sliced potatoes and onions in spattering bear grease. He inspected the large slab of meat in the lamp light; blowing across it several times and wiping it with his hand to get the hair off, he plopped the dripping flesh into the pan. The meat sizzled like a red-hot horse shoe as it's plunged into the quenching tub, and its strange aroma filled the cabin. "Pull up that keg," he invited, "and set a spell; may as well fill your meat bag while I do. Then I can tell ye the *ins* and *outs* of my hunt."

I had never been Gid's guest for a meal, and was a little apprehensive, but I consented. I knew his story would be worth the hearing, and anyway, I was starved. When the meal was nearly ready to serve, Gid lit another lantern and handed it to me.

"I'd be obliged if you'd go to the well and fetch my plate and cup and a pitcher of that good cold Adam's ale." I wondered about the plate and cup which he kept in the well bucket. When I returned, he explained.

"See, I keep my plate and cup down deep where they stay cool; that way I never have to wash 'em when I'm done, and they stay sanitatious." I marveled at his healthful practices. Gid stepped to the single board nailed to his cabin wall that served as a shelf and grabbed his other plate. He wiped the dust from it with his shirt tail and set it before me. As I pulled up to the table, I swept its surface clean of crumbs and a dozen ants with a broad sweep of my hand. "Go easy, Pilgrim!" exclaimed Gid, "I'll thank you for not treatin' my ants so rough. They's just tryin' to make an honest livin', and they wasn't done cleanin' up yet." Gid dished out the grub and we dug in. The meat was palatable, but I couldn't identify it by taste.

"Painter," said Gid. I had never eaten anything feline, and felt a bit squeamish. Between bites, I prodded my host to begin his story.

"I tell ye, I thought I was a gone beaver," he smacked. "See, ol' Hez Forrest had seen a passel o' catamount tracks by his sheep pen and finally figgered where his animals had been disappearin' to. He knows I like to chase down bandits like that renegade painter, and since I'd once got the raccoons that was killin' his chickens, he called me in to help him again.

"Well, I tracked that mutton thief to his lair way up on Firebrand Pass. Heck, he put down a trail a kid or a flatlander could 'a' followed in the dark - almost like he was darin' me to catch him. Why, he'd left tufts o' wool snagged on branches and roots, and he hunkered down two or three times to chaw some more from the carcass. Anyway, I saw where he'd crawled in under this hugeacious glacier-stopper of a boulder. I walked around lookin' for a second doorway and found one a couple of rods away, so I rolled a big rock onto it and returned to the main entrance. Pass me that-there pitcher again, will ye?"

Gid slurped a long draught from his cup, wiped his mouth on his sleeve and belched with gusto before continuing.

"I wasn't about to abandon chase just because the thief had beat me to his hideout. Besides, the thought o' rasslin' with a painter in his cave was kind of excitin' to me. So I put fresh primin' in Centershot and begun to slither in under that rock. I barely had room to wiggle, and I had to push the rifle on the ground before me. I was blockin' the only light, so it was dark as the bottom o' my well. After ten or fifteen feet, why it opened up in there so I could get to my knees. I waited for the attack, but it didn't come. After a minute or two, my eyes began to pick out a few details. A shaft o' light came in from a crack overhead, and the entry way let some daylight in. I swan, I never saw nothin' like it! The small chamber I was in was like an entry way to a bigger cave. I couldn't see into the other room yet, but my mouth dropped open at the furnishin's all around me: an arrangement of skulls from sheep, cows, dogs, horses, deer, raccoons, and all kinds of other four-leggeds, tame and wild. Why, this was the varmint's trophy room, and I wish to be shot if he didn't have more keepsakes in his diggin's than I have in mine! I saw he didn't have no human skulls yet, but I figgered he was lookin' forward to his first.

"When I saw the evidence o' all that depreda-
tiousness, I got my bowels in an uproar and resolved to
do manly combat with the varmint. I stepped real
cautious into the next chamber, and listened for the
critter. It's cold, and blacker 'n night; I don't hear
nothin' but a couple o' bats squeekin' overhead and a
drip-plop from a trickle o' water somewheres. I figger
I can take my fire kit and kindle some tinder to see
where the bandit lies; then I see his eyes just a second
too late, when I'm reachin' for my tinder box. The devil
screams and pounces on me in a second and I know I'm
goin' under."

Here Gid stopped for a minute and checked the
fire in the cookstove. He had put on too much wood and
the air in the cabin was becoming hot and close. He
fidgeted a moment with the stove, opened his grimy
shirt and scratched, and sat down to finish his meal.
He appeared to have forgotten the thread of his tale. I
couldn't stand the suspense any longer. "Well? What
happened? Did you shoot the critter?"

"Heck no, I didn't shoot him. I never had time to
raise and fire. What in Tunket do you *think* happened?
The devil pounced on me and killed me outright!" Here
Gid exploded into a loud guffaw, spewing chewed
potatoes like a charge of birdshot from my 20-gauge
blanket gun. Gid wiped the greasy shrapnel from the
table onto the floor to join remnants of meals past. I felt
like I'd blindly swallowed his line, and shot him a glance
which he correctly interpreted as a signal to level with
me.

"Naw, he didn't quite kill me. But he knocked me
to the ground and I lost my rifle. We rassled for maybe
a minute, and I knew I was in trouble. I'd never seen
such a tarnacious catamount, and I believe he could 'a'

done me in any second he wished to. But I think he wanted to play with me a little before killing me, the way all cats do. Well, I figgered, I may lose this tussle, but not till I've showed my grit. So I make a lunge for him, and in the dark it's kind o' hard to keep coordinated, 'cause he's springin' for me at the same instant. We meet in the middle, and through bad luck, I pop in headfirst, right between them fangs. The infidel commences to swallowin' me as hard as he can, and little by little, I get squeezed into his belly. It's mighty dark and close, but at least it's warm, I think to myself. I swan, that was a worrisome perdickament.

"Well, after a while, the painter started to move. I could feel his belly hangin' low, movin' from side to side. It felt like I was layin' in a hammock swayin' in the wind. Then he flop down and begin to crawl out o' the den. I could feel him squeezin' through and wondered if he was goin' to make it. Once clear, he ambled a couple hunnerd yards and lay down to digest. My mind's racin' to figger out a way to escape, and I tried a couple ideers one by one. First I took my firekit and kindled all my tinder, as I'd hoped to do earlier. In the light, I see several dead animals - includin' one o' Hez's sheep - crowded around, waitin' to be digested, and I get a little discouraged. The fire makes plenty o' smoke, too, and the painter sneeze and cough most beautifully, but I'm *still* caught. I get treated kinda rough when he sneeze, what with bones and carcasses flyin' about his insides. My tinder's used up, so I draw my butcher knife, figgerin' I can cut him open from the inside and escape; but the blade just clanks against his innards, and I realize the devil has a *cast iron stummock* ! And he had to, by Tunket; why, you should have seen the junk in there, but you know what kind o' carrion and such them critters goozle up.

"Well, finally I saw that his medicine was stronger 'n mine, and I resigned myself to goin' under. I stretched out as cozy as I could under the circumstances, fluffed up a ol' owl he'd et up whole, set my head on it, and closed my eyes. As an afterthought, I decided there was no need to go under with my mockersons on, so I kicked 'em off to be more comfortable.

"Shortly I feel the critter's stummock begin to crawl. He stirs a bit in his bed. Then the stummock begin to buck in earnest, and before you could say hush to a duck, he's took with the heaves. I feel like I'm on a wild horse. Lookin' down between my feet, I see daylight openin' up, and I realize I'm about to get evicted. But before I go, I reach over my head and grab the tip o' his tail from the inside. When he finally spews me out o' there, I hang on, and I wish to be kicked to death by grasshoppers if I don't *snap* that catamount teetotally inside-out! That's his hide I dumped by the door tonight, and we jus' et one o' his steaks. I swan that painter had stummock for all kinds o' rot, but he couldn't take the likes o' me without my mocs! So ye see, a cleaner man would 'a' gone under, and I *owe my life* to runnin' out o' soap back in '43."

I realized I had just been taken in again, and it was up to me to filter out as much of the story as I chose to believe. I was done with my meal, and Gid reached for my plate. Banging it four or five times on the floor, he whistled loudly. Lightnin', his arthritic and nearly deaf hound dog, clicked across the puncheon floor and lapped the plate clean. Gid replaced the plate on the shelf without further pretense of cleaning it.

By now the stove had burned down to red-hot coals; the cabin was uncomfortably hot, and sweat beaded on our foreheads. Gid's presence had expanded somewhat in the close atmosphere and I found my stomach feeling mighty queersome.

Gid leaned back in his chair with his feet resting across a corner of the kitchen table. "Yep, that made for a tarnal rough day o' huntin', and I hope never to bring home the bacon that way agin. It feels mighty good to relax in my own diggin's after such a tough hike." So saying, Gid kicked his moccasins off. Instantly my eyes watered and I could scarcely see; I imagined that the brass hardware on his old rifle turned a darker shade of black, and I thought I heard the woodstove gasp for air. For my part, I had just endured the yarn of a man breaking free from inside a catamount, and now the catamount inside me began to clamor for release. My stomach rolled and heaved, and I excused myself saying that I had to return home to put the animals into the barn.

"Thank you for the - gulp - meal, Gid. I'm glad you're - gulp - fine. I'll see you again soon." I made it to the door in time to quell the catamount's uprising. As I hurried off in the darkness, stumbling over the huge hide Gid had deposited, I wondered if he had intentionally signaled a close to our visit, and just how much of his tale I could swallow.

Eric A. Bye

A PARTNERSHIP

Eric A. Bye

Last May, a little before Spring turkey season, I was sneaking through the woods trying to locate a flock that had been reported in the area, when I spotted a rough-clad stranger making his way toward me along the same ridge. He carried a long rifle, horn, possibles pouch, and a small stone jug. I could tell by the stealth of his tread that he was reading sign. He had an awkward gait, but clearly he was no newcomer to the ways of the forest. I figured that he too was in search of turkeys in anticipation of the season and that we might share our discoveries with one another. We approached to within a few yards of each other, and for a moment we both appeared hesitant to break the stillness of the woods with human speech. As we nodded silently to each other, the stranger placed the jug between us, made a furtive check of the priming in the pan of his rifle, and stepped back a few paces. I glanced around quickly to be sure that my voice wouldn't startle any game and was the first to speak.

"Howdy," I began. "You seen--," I choked on my words, for before I could finish, the stranger leveled his rifle at me; his eyes gleamed and there was a strange excitement in his voice as he commanded, "Pilgrim, reach for that jug and take a good draft!" What else could I do but obey? I paused for an instant to sniff the contents before touching the jug to my lips. My host repeated, "Drink!"

I took four swallows of the fellow's 'shine - or rather, the same mouthful four times. The concoction, which I later learned contained a plug of tobacco and a handful of hot peppers, made me shudder like a retriever shaking the water off. That 'shine seared my mouth and throat and made the hair on the back of my neck bristle, and I swan it felt like lightning was shooting through my nose. After a minute I could gasp a faint "Waugh!", whereupon the stranger chuckled once and nodded as he handed me his rifle. "Now," he said, "you hold the gun on me whilst I takes a drink."

After that introductory ceremony, we indeed exchanged information about turkey sign and hunting in general. One thing led to another and our conversation, still rather hoarse on my part, turned to other topics such as firelocks, and the relative merits of rifles and smoothbores. Despite the inauspicious introduction, we had a few interests and tastes in common, excepting of course the example of a moment ago.

As long as I came to know the man, I never knew his real name; but like most buckskinners with the hair o' the bear in them and who had seen the elephant and the lizard, he had a nickname. He responded to the fitting name of Plenty-Coup-Coup.

Plenty-Coup-Coup confided that he was looking to strike up a partnership, having recently lost his home and possessions. When I met him, he was making his way to town to try to find some job, but he would have been as out of place there as a hen in a fox den, and about as vulnerable. For savvy though he was in the woods, I had reason to believe he wouldn't last long in the settlements. Clearly he preferred to remain in the woods, and I judged that only dire emergency would force him to consider moving into civilized diggings.

"How did you lose your cabin, Plenty-Coup-Coup?" I asked. "I reckon it must have been something bad." He seemed hesitant to speak.

"I ain't inclined to tell 'less'n you promises not to scoff."

"Pardner, I take no amusement from the misfortune of others. You're right; if you're not comfortable telling me, better keep it to yourself."

"Well, all right, then," he began, shyly at first. "A couple weeks ago my ol' coon dog got too old and sick to walk. That had been comin' on for a year or more, and I should o' been more ready for it. But I swan he were the best friend I had, and mebbe I just warn't willin' to give over to it. But I knowed he wouldn't last another month, and I hated to see 'im jest layin' around all crippled up. I couldn't shoot 'im or jest haul 'im out t' the swamp and let the coyotes or tree-foxes git 'im. So I hit on a ideer. I needed to blast out a stump from the corner o' my clearin', about a hunnerd yard from my cabin. So I figgered, why not kill two birds with one stone? I'll put the dog and dynamite together and give that rascal a head start to dog heaven. An' that ways, I don't have to see him for the last time through rifle sights nor bury him, and I gets two uses out o' my stick o' dynamite.

"I gave 'im ever' chance to recover. I patted 'im, tweaked 'im, put meat in front o' his nose, and never got nary a response. He jest lay there like a ol' bag o' bones, scarc'ly breathin'. So I figgered the time had come. I took a couple pieces o' rawhide and tied my stick o' dynamite onto his underside. Still nary a sign o' life from 'im. Then I carried 'im out and laid 'im in amongst the roots o' that big ol' stump where the blast'd do the most good. He's still jest as limp as a ol' mokerson. So I pats 'im a couple o' times and bids him fare-thee-well and told him he'd been a good dog, and to enjoy his reward and we'd meet one day on t'other side.

"The way I tied that dynamite on 'im, see, the fuse stuck out backwards betwixt his hind legs. I lit it and ran lickity-clippity back toward my cabin to take shelter and watch it blow. I got jest halfway there when what do I see but my crippled dog racin' past me at full speed, bowlegged, with one tail between his legs and another spittin' sparks like an axe blade on a grind stone! Well, sir, away he run straight for his favorite hidin' place, where only a dog could go, right underneath my cabin.

"Get out o' there, you mangy son of a sea sarpent!" I yells, forgettin' right fast my attachment to the poor devil. I skidded to a halt, not knowin' which way to turn. I ran forwards and backwards and left and right, and ended up dashin' back to that stump, double-checkin' real quick to be sure that dog hadn't left the dynamite there. So I dives behind the stump, the only safe place in the whole clearin', jest as my cabin goes sky-high. It rained kindlin' for five minutes, but I got no place to use it now."

Plenty-Coup-Coup suggested that we could team up for some hunting and trap-line work, and I agreed reluctantly; it was a risk to team up with a stranger, but I knew I could use the help. Plenty-Coup-Coup could handle a canoe, cook, sing some voyageur songs, and read sign far more easily than the printed word. He was colorful company and competent in the woods, but I was to learn that his bad luck with the cabin was not uncharacteristic.

One day, we were paddling together to check some sets on our trap line. As we moved toward shore, I asked Plenty-Coup-Coup to pass me my possibles bag and horn, which I had lain on the bottom of the canoe. He stretched to hand them to me, but as he back-paddled to ease our landing, he fumbled and dropped horn and bag overboard into deep water. He acted mortified, and instantly dove into the river to recover the lost goods. In his haste, he plunged in with his buckskins and possibles. I waited on the bank for him to surface. After a minute, I was concerned; after two, I concluded with alarm that he'd drowned in the attempt to rectify his blunder. There was nothing to do but dive in and try to recover the corpse.

The water at that point was about ten feet deep and fairly clear. I could see Plenty-Coup-Coup plainly as I came up on him. And the rascal blushed, for he hadn't drowned at all, but was standing on the river bottom intently trying to pour the powder from my horn into his! Bubbles exploded from his mouth as he tried to offer an explanation. I merely pointed to the surface and indicated that we should return to land.

"Plenty-Coup-Coup," I panted, "if you're out of powder, just ask and I'll give you some! Now you get a fire started to dry out our plunder while I take a quick hike through the woods to see if I can find a black birch and a sassafras so we can make some hot tea." And peeling off my wet buckskins, I changed into my breech-cloth and entered the adjoining woods.

I returned in a short while and was gratified to see the curl of smoke indicating that Plenty-Coup-Coup had managed to start a fire. Clad only in his breech-cloth, he was huddled over the flames to warm himself and to dry a buckskin shirt on an improvised rack of green branches.

As I approached, there erupted a roar and a black cloud which shot skyward from the fire pit. Plenty-Coup-Coup was bowled over backwards. I rushed up, helped him to his feet, and discovered that he was unharmed, except for some wildly singed hair on his torso and face. His wide eyes looked like glowing embers in a smoldering brush pile, for smoke still rose from his tangled hair and beard. A mouth emerged from the featureless, soot-covered face as he spat cinders and wiped his lips, to offer an explanation.

"I was dryin' a shirt over the fire and figgered maybe I could dry our powder and salvage it. I felt kind o' bad, you know, gettin' all our powder wet. So I poured the paste outen our horns and spread it on the shirt over the fire. I was goin' to roast it dry, but I reckon it got past done, 'cause when I went to stir it, off it went."

I looked at the shirt which had a big hole burned in it and now lay smouldering in the remains of the fire, and remarked, "Too bad you ruined your fine buckskin shirt in the bargain, companyero."

He glanced self-consciously at me and replied, "I'm sorry, capitaine, but that shirt be your'n."

So I said, "Coup-Coup," for I was beginning to prefer the abbreviated version of his name, "there have not been many instances in our partnership where I have been moved to give you the shirt off my back, but this is one." And I promptly took possession of his shirt. Coup-Coup salvaged a few of the shreds from the fire-pit and tried them on. They left most of his upper body exposed.

"Well, capitaine," he said contritely, "hit ain't much, but I'll make do till I kin make me another one." And as Coup-Coup bent for his tin cup, he shot instantly erect, slapped himself in the middle of the back and danced a couple of frantic steps, as a man slaps at a yellow-jacket, for a previously undetected hot spot in the shirt had made contact. He glanced sheepishly at me and by way of apology for his bungling, offered to rekindle the fire for our tea - a task which he accomplished without further mishap.

Just before snowfall that year we fell in with a band of fur trappers we'd met by chance. We were all headed in the same direction and we thought it wise to join forces for a few days. The first night, the temperature fell through the floor and a bitter wind blew out of the North. We prepared to sleep with our capotes and blankets, for by sundown it was clear that we were in for a real knee-knocker. So we all built fires to thaw the ground where we planned to sleep; scraping away the embers and the top layer of soil, we buried some rocks we had heated in the fire. Those would keep us warm through most of the night. The only problem was our feet. We decided to keep a large fire in the center of a circle; each man would sleep with a fifteen-foot log next to him, and every time he awoke in the night, he would push his log a little farther into the fire. That way, the fire would be fed all night and no one would have to leave the robes to fetch fuel. We finally lay down in a circle around the fire, like points on a sundial. Before long, men's snoring became louder than the hiss and crackle of the fire.

          You know what it's like to sleep in a penetrating cold. You get into a single comfortable position and you can't budge, for any movement puts you into unheated territory. Plenty Coup-Coup, who was normally a restless sleeper, was more agitated than normal that night. Some of his horrible squeezin's, taken before hitting the robes in order to warm his insides, apparently worked on him. Though asleep, he continually twisted and jerked, sometimes flailing about with his arms and calling out. Unconsciously, he advanced his log into the fire every half hour or so with the result that it caught fire over several feet of its length and crept out the opposite end of the fire pit toward a snoring trapper. At that point, Coup-Coup unfortunately gave such a spasmodic push on his log that it scudded the remaining distance toward the unsuspecting sleeper. The flames thus applied to the man's legs and posterior caused him immediately to spring awake, yelling as if he were already captured and burning at the stake. At this alarm, we all jumped up out of our robes, grabbed our rifles and dashed into the shadows to take the anticipated attack. We shivered and our teeth clacked together like bare bones before we deduced what had happened. We returned to bed badly agitated and froze for the rest of the night. The next morning, the other trappers parted company with us before breakfast. I made a mental note never to sleep on the opposite side of the campfire from Coup-Coup.

Plenty Coup-Coup and I trapped and hunted together for much of that year. He was pretty good company, but after a while his quirks became bothersome, and I wasn't too heartbroken when he decided to quit. Here's how it happened.

We were stalking through the woods when we both spotted a catamount asleep in the sun. The critter was *facing us directly* and offered a demanding target. Plenty-Coup-Coup shouldered Old Killdeer and peered through the sights at the feline head. At the precise instant he touched off the shot, before the report had even reached the painter, that cat opened his mouth in a wide yawn, spun around with lightning speed, and bounded off in the opposite direction as if nothing had happened. I turned to Plenty-Coup-Coup to remark in astonishment over his apparent miss and found the poor devil stretched out on the ground with a bullet crease alongside his head! You see his shot had entered through the catamount's mouth as it yawned; the ball passed harmlessly along the critter's gut and exited through the hindmost orifice, being directed back at Plenty-Coup-Coup as the cat wheeled and bounded off! It's mighty lucky for Plenty-Coup-Coup that the cat was an older one and not quite as quick as most of his kind, for if he had been, that shot would have caught my partner right between the eyes.

Plenty-Coup-Coup came to in a minute and shook his head in disbelief. He had scarcely survived his latest blunder - attempting a head shot on a painter - and declared that he had no appetite to tempt fate further. And so, wishing me well and admonishing me to take only broadside shots at such targets, he shook my hand and left my service. He returned to his clearing where he's built a new cabin and now scratches out a scant but safe living from the soil.

He's left a void I'd like to fill. I hadn't figured I'd grown so dependent on his help, but maybe that just indicates he was more useful than I tend to give him credit for. If you can cook, handle a canoe, sing cadence in voyageur songs, and read sign, I'll consider your application to join me for the next season.

PROSPECTING ON THE WINNEANIMUS

*You know what it's like in the Yukon wild
when it's sixty-nine below;
When the ice worms wriggle their purple heads
through the crust of the pale blue snow;
When pine trees crack like little guns in the
silence of the wood,
And the icicles hang down like tusks under
the parka hood.*
                    Robert Service
                    The Ballad of Blasphemous Bill

We'd been at the Nipintuk placer mine on the
Winneanimus River in Alaska's interior for a year or
more. That's long enough to get shed of the stigma of
being a cheechako, or greenhorn, and earn a reputation as a savvy hiveranno, at least if you work at it. We
loved life in the wilderness; there's no greater majesty
on earth than the Northern Wilds, but you've got to
respect it and continually watch yourself or it will
simply overpower you.

Now it seemed that the Nipintuk's days were
numbered, as it produced less gold each month. My
Indian friends, Athabasca Jack and Tah-weah, and I all
dreaded the prospect of returning to civilized diggin's to
find work. We'd all tried that before, and it didn't take
us long to sour on life in the settlements. Jack and Tah-
weah, lean and brown as yearling grizzlies, had been
raised in the bush and cut their teeth on caribou and
salmon. Civilization held no appeal for us, and since a
steady hand with a rifle and wilderness survival skills
are of no use in the settlements, we had little to offer to
that tame kind of life. We were better suited to tundra
than to pavement, and we agreed to stay in the wilderness at all costs.

There wasn't much to do in camp, so when we proposed to reconnoitre for yellower pastures farther up the river, the boss gave us the go-ahead. We hoped to get closer to the source of the scant gold that was washing down to us and maybe discover a new site for our operations. So early last October, we packed up our provisions; armed with our trusted flintlocks and collective knowledge of the wilderness, we set off on foot. Our plan was to return in about three weeks, before Winter came to stay.

After about ten days of trekking, we were on the banks of the Winneanimus about eighty miles above the Nipintuk, where none of us had ever been before. The river was becoming shallower and ran flat and slow for as far as we could see, so we resolved to save some tedious steps through the deepening snow cover and construct a bull boat. We knew we had to build our boat before we got too far into the hills to find game for hides or saplings for a frame. We had the good fortune to intersect a caribou trail a couple of miles beyond the nearest ridge, and in a few short hours we had enough fresh meat for the remainder of our expedition and the hides we needed for our bull boat. We spent the better part of a day cutting saplings and lacing them into a wickiup shape, which when covered with hides and inverted, would provide our water transportation. We worked caribou fat into the seams to keep the river at bay and prepared for a test run. We stowed our gear on the bottom of the boat to provide ballast and installed a platform to stand on as we poled our way upstream. The bull boat lacked a keel and as a result, it seemed to stagger and reel upstream like a drunken water bug. After a while, though, we were able to coordinate our poling to the point where we were making better time on water than we could have done on shore. The boat remained a very jittery and precarious craft; however, as we got used to it, we appreciated her usefulness and we shortly recognized her as an integral part of the team. We fondly christened her the *Peapod.*

After another three days of poling, the Winne-animus became so swift that we could no longer make any headway. Our only course was to beach the boat and continue on foot once again. We anticipated being out only a few more days before beginning the quick return trip. We wanted to explore a little more deeply into the canyons and hills we could see several miles ahead, and since we could look forward to an easy trip down river, we felt that the construction of our boat had actually bought us a few extra days to spend on our mission.

Since we now depended upon the *Peapod* for our trip back to the Nipintuk, we took pains to assure her safe storage for the few days that we would be separated from her. We feared that a hungry wolf or arctic fox might gnaw the hides if we didn't protect her, and it was also possible that other humans abroad in the wilderness would appropriate her for their use if we didn't conceal her carefully. So we filled her full of rocks from the shore and sank her in about four feet of water near a large boulder that would serve as a landmark. Then we pressed on into the hills to see if there was any hope for the success of our mission.

We hiked and explored the hills without any sign of gold. We believed there was plenty to be found, but we'd arrived too late to beat the snows. Reluctantly we called off the search and headed back towards the *Peapod* for our ride downriver.

We were still a day's hike away from the boat when we all remarked on an impending shift in the weather. I could feel in my joints that something was going to change. The temperature plummeted during the night and several times we awoke, shivering, to the sound of the wind howling down from the north. In the morning, the snow and wind made traveling difficult, but it was too cold to stay put. We were anxious to drop out of the highlands to the warmer level of the river and we knew we had to get under way before the river froze solid for the winter.

Upon reaching the river we were crestfallen to discover that it had indeed frozen. The wind drove the snow with such fury that we could scarcely see the boulder marking the spot where we had sunk the *Peapod.* We made a token attempt at hacking away the ice where we thought she lay, hoping we could recover her and push her over the ice until we found open, navigable water - if there was any left between there and the Nipintuk. But we soon despaired of freeing her - our bull boat was icebound and useless until spring, and we now faced the bleak prospect of a grueling hike back to the Nipintuk. An overland hike would be the shortest distance, but there were mountains to over-come, and with the wind and snow, it would be too foolhardy to attempt that route. Our only chance was to stick to the frozen river, so we dejectedly resumed our trek on the surface of the Winneanimus.

As we walked, the ice boomed and cracked under our feet like rifle fire. As anyone knows who has spent time on the ice this is a normal result of expan-sion and settling of the ice, so it did not alarm us. Fortunately, the wind was at our backs, for the travel was grueling enough without the sting of snow in our faces. Our mukluks were smooth as hard-soled moc-casins on the bottom, affording us scant purchase on the slick, frozen trail, and we kept on our feet with difficulty. In fact, so precarious was our footing that we linked arms to support each other and reduce the number of inevitable falls we would otherwise have taken. This also served to keep us together, for to become separated in such weather conditions would have been very dangerous.

We had trekked perhaps a half-dozen miles in that fashion when fatigue, cold and the weather began to take their toll. When Tah-weah, linked arm and arm between Athabasca Jack and me, lost his balance, he took all three of us down. We landed CRASH on our backs at the same instant. To our horror, the ice shattered beneath us and down we plunged! But instead of an icy and surely fatal bath, we plummeted a fathom through space and landed on the river bottom! Our packs broke our fall, so we escaped serious injury. I bumped my head a bit on impact, and Jack got a small cut on his forehead from a piece of falling ice. Otherwise, we were unhurt. We looked around us in amazement at the ice-domed corridor. Above us, the wind and snow continued to howl past the opening we had made with our fall; the noise was like a steam locomotive whistle, rising and falling with the changing wind speed. The river was empty of water below its skin of ice! The freeze had come in so quickly that the surface had frozen almost instantly and the river water had continued to drain out from beneath it. The tributaries and watershed that fed the river had frozen solid so quickly that there was no water to replenish it. We were in a strange subterranean corridor fully protected from the elements above and twenty degrees warmer than the environment from which we had just dropped. And this corridor led straight down to the Nipintuk. It didn't take much deliberation to resolve to continue our journey under the ice rather than on top of it.

The floor of the river was wet and rocky, with puddles here and there, so walking was still difficult. Enough daylight filtered through the ice above to illuminate our passageway. The dampness and eerie, flat light were chilling. As we walked on, it seemed that the ceiling was rising - but of course the floor was dropping as the river got deeper. We had gone a couple hundred yards from our entry point into the river when Athabasca Jack, who was in the lead, exclaimed, "Well, will you looky here!" Tah-weah and I scurried up to see a beautiful two pound brook trout that had been left behind by the river. It was just gasping its last, so we figured that the retreating waters were not too far ahead of us. Several yards beyond, we found a half-dozen more trout in similar straits. We were reminded that we hadn't eaten a bite since breakfast and decided to try to cook up the fish. We had plenty of tinder and charcloth for a fire, but dry fuel presented a major problem. We spied some branches sticking downward through the ice and knew that a tree had once collapsed from the banks above and leaned over the water. Its lower branches had been captured in the freeze. By hacking with our tomahawks we were able to free a few branches from the grip of the ice and kindle a fire to cook our trout, which we spitted on a branch. We had to build the cook fire directly under the hole we had chopped to get the firewood, in order for the smoke to escape without filling our cavern. At that, our fire was a poor one, and the fish were more smoked than cooked. The heat from the fire caused the ice above it to melt and drop on us like rain, while the wind roared down the hole. Icicles began to form above, and as they grew they took on the appearance of stalactites, completing the decor of our bizarre cavern. In all, it was an uncomfortable spot, so we resolved to move on as quickly as possible. To complicate matters, the combination of dripping water and inrushing Arctic wind from the opening at our lunch site made for a thin coating of ice underfoot. That would probably not last once we got beyond the reach of the wind, but we immediately had to contend with a steep, sloping ledge about twenty yards in length. Stretching the entire width of the river, the surface was polished dance floor smooth from centuries of scouring by the waters of the Winneanimus. This was covered by a slick skin of new ice, and it dropped away from us at an alarming angle, around a bend and into a field of forbidding boulders and shadows. In the eerie half-light under the ice, we proceeded tentatively and soberly. Tah-weah, in a flash of inspiration, suggested that we create some traction by lacing the fish skeletons to the soles of our mukluks. That worked for a few steps, but because trout skeletons aren't made to stand up to such use, we quickly slipped and found ourselves sliding down the slope, ending once again in a heap on the river's floor. Fortunately we all reached the foot of the chute without injury.

"It's a good thing we didn't leave anything behind at the campfire, because we couldn't scale that slope again if our lives depended on it," I observed. On we trudged.

The light overhead seemed to brighten after a short while, so we figured that the storm had abated. As we hiked onward, Athabaska Jack stopped almost in mid-stride and turned to Tah-weah and me. "You know," he said, "I been thinkin' about your last remark about gettin' back up that slippery ledge, and you're right. We don't know what the weather's like up there, and we'd be in a turrible fix if that sun thawed out the drainage that supplies this river!"

Jack's observation made us all uneasy; what if yesterday's storm wasn't the true onset of winter, but only a false beginning? On we trudged, resolved to get back to the surface as quickly as possible and deal with the elements above, rather than the threat of a flash flood below.

Unfortunately the ceiling of ice was now about four feet over our heads, and if earlier experiences were any indication, it was probably at least a foot thick. The river seemed to be passing through a gorge of some sort, for the sides were vertical and offered no handhold to permit approaching the underside of the ice, which at that point was nearly as clear as glass.

The light dimmed momentarily as a shadow passed quickly overhead. We all glanced up and saw the silhouette of a tremendous bear standing on the ice above us. His head grew bigger and came into clearer focus as he lowered it to the ice, peering and sniffing. His breath frosted the ice, and he moved his ponderous head to the side for a clearer look. We didn't know if he could see us. He pounced hard on the ice with his forepaws, and we recoiled as the ice boomed above our heads. The thought of having a ravenous bear loosed among us in our subterranean confinement froze my blood. The bear raked his huge claws over the ice and tried several times to gnaw through it. To our ears the grinding sound he made was like the crunching of our bones in his terrible maw. We exchanged worried glances and instinctively checked the priming of our rifles and felt for our belt knives. That's the closest any of us had been to a live bear, and we were grateful for the ice barrier. We watched as the bear lifted his head, tested the wind, and moved on, his heavy footsteps receding upstream. We continued nervously in the opposite direction, still searching for an opportunity to return to the surface. But now we didn't know if we were safer above or below the ice.

Of course, we were mindful of the original purpose of our expedition all the while, and we continually watched the ground under our feet. We realized that few men are granted such an inside look at a river known for the gold it carries, so every few yards we turned over rocks and inspected handfuls of sand. Our luck took a quick turn for the better, and it seemed almost too good to be true; I bent over and, whooping triumphantly, held out a couple of good sized nuggets for Jack and Tah-weah to inspect. Shortly thereafter they both found more, which they cached in their pockets for the return trip. We congratulated each other and promised ourselves a toast later on. Despite our good fortune, we remained preoccupied and uneasy about our present situation below the ice.

The farther we traveled, the harder we panted. Our hearts raced and we felt light-headed. Initially I thought this was due to our finding the gold, but we had found gold before without experiencing such symptoms, and I was puzzled. Although I couldn't think clearly, I had a flash of insight which may have saved our lives. "Hey, do you feel strange?" I asked my companions. Jack replied, "Yeah, I'm plumb played out. I'm so tuckered I could drop right here." Tah-weah admitted to difficulty in catching his breath. "I know!" I exclaimed. "There's not enough air in here! The farther we go from the opening in the ice, the thinner the air gets! Come on - we've got to go back to some air!"

It was distasteful to retrace our steps, but we could think of no alternative. We returned to the foot of the ledge we'd slid down and confirmed our earlier judgement about the impossibility of scaling its icy surface. But nearby we spotted a pile of large boulders that allowed us to climb nearly to the underside of the ice and begin chopping away at it with our tomahawks and knives. The work was painfully slow, with ice fragments showering us at every stroke. The ice was rock hard and thick, and once the labor started, all our energy and attention were devoted to piercing an escape hole through the ceiling of ice. Our necks and shoulders ached from the awkward labor. In desperation, Jack suggested that we perforate the ice by firing bullet holes through the ceiling in a pattern that would allow us to connect the holes by chopping. We took turns shooting. The report was deafening, and the black powder smoke filled the cavern. We each shot twice and took turns climbing to the top of the biggest boulder to chop. At least we now had some small holes which afforded fresh air and encouragement to finish the job. Jack was chopping away and finally cleared a hole large enough to poke his head through to the world above. "It's still blowing", he called down, "but the sky has cleared, and it looks a damsite better than it does down here".

Jack eventually made a hole large enough to squeeze through. Tah-weah climbed up and passed our rifles to Jack while I watched from the floor of the river bed. Suddenly a horrifying roar echoed through the tunnel, and at the top of the slick ledge I spotted an enormous bear - undoubtedly the same one we had seen through the ice. Probably he had smelled the remains of our trout lunch and entered the empty river in search of more. Now he was tracking us by the fish scent on the soles of our boots. He looked gaunt and mean, as if the freeze had surprised him without a meal and a den for a long sleep. He figured he was within striking distance of his next meal. My rifle was above ground and unloaded anyway, so I drew my belt knife and yelled to Tah-weah to clear the smoke stack as I was coming up! His feet disappeared up the hole just as I scrambled to the top of the boulders and prepared to jump into the world above. My last vision of the scene below was the enraged bruin careening down the icy slope and spinning like a top as he struck the boulders at my feet.

Up on the surface of the ice, we heard the bear bawl with rage at being denied a meal. We hastily began to recharge our rifles, resolving not to be caught without loaded guns again. As we did so, the bear gained the top of the boulders and stuck his head out of the hole to roar at us; fortunately he could not squeeze through the opening. Down his head went, as his paws reached up to claw away at the edges of the hole. When he poked his head up again, I remarked that he presented a target like we were used to at the turkey shoots back home. Jack shouldered his fusil and approached the bear for a closer look, at which the beast redoubled his efforts to squeeze through and grab us. As the bruin thrust with his hind legs, he broke loose a section of ice in a wide circumference around the hole and his neck. He was now thoroughly stuck, and as he flailed madly about with his head, he crashed back into the chasm with a tremendously heavy collar of thick ice wedged clear down to his shoulders. He was pilloried in such a fashion that he could only churn with his hind legs. He shook and bawled and thrashed about on the river bottom, but he couldn't free himself. From our vantage point above, only the bear's bottom presented itself. Jack seemed less inclined to shoot the bear now that he wasn't so game a target, and he was understandably averse to going back down for a better shot. He advised moving on as quickly as possible. "After all, if he manages to break that ice collar free, or if he melts it enough to slip out of it, he'll be coming out of that hole like a cannon shot."

We double timed for a couple of miles to put some distance between us and the bear, frequently glancing over our shoulders to be sure we weren't pursued; but despite the incentive we had to cover ground, we soon found ourselves too knackered to continue at that pace. The wind was still strong at our backs, and we feared the cheerless need to travel some four or five days to Nipintuk on scant rations and energy. We didn't know if we could make it. The situation was serious, and we called a grim council in the lee of a boulder to determine our plan of action.

We knew we would never be found by any search party or random passers-by. Our only hope remained getting back to the mine under our own power. As I paced back and forth contemplating our predicament, I accidentally stepped out of the lee with my back to the wind. A powerful gust fairly picked me up and blew me ten feet across the ice. "I've got it!", I cried above the wind. "Look, we don't have the strength or provisions to attempt an overland trip, and the watercourse we had hoped to ride is now useless for navigation. But we can sail home!"

So saying, I untied my blanket coat and lashed each bottom corner to the laces of my high-topped mukluks. Then I slid my rifle into the sleeves of my capote and held it crosswise over the back of my shoulders. By spreading my legs and arms bat-like so that the capote was stretched taut between them, I was able to catch enough wind to be propelled across the ice on the smooth soles of my mukluks. It worked! How we did skim across the crystal pavement of the Winneanimus! The wind continued unabated from the north,

supplying all the propulsion we needed. With experience, we were able to control both our speed and
direction. To slow down, we brought our legs together
or crouched to catch less wind; to turn, we merely lifted
one foot and let the wind pivot us. Why, when the river
turned and the wind hit us obliquely rather than
square from behind, we could even tack by bending and
twisting from the waist. Not only did we have great
sport at it, we covered ground at what I estimate to be
between twenty and twenty-five miles an hour. You
should have seen us! No ballroom dancer, no Dawson
stripper ever cut a more graceful form than we did as
we bent and turned and stepped along the frozen
surface of the Winneanimus on the two October days it
took us to return to the Nipintuk. We made just one
cold camp on the way back as we sailed into the long
night while the wind lasted. I swan I'll remember as
long as I live the feel of the ice under my feet, the push
of the wind, and the picture of Athabasca Jack and
Tah-weah scudding along under the midnight aurora
borealis!

Hooting for joy we sailed into camp just as our
wide-eyed colleagues were bending into the wind on
their way to the mess hall for a supper of pea soup and
galette. To us it was ambrosia. We had returned from
a severe trial in the frozen wilderness, and with the gold
we'd tucked into our pockets in the bowels of the hollow
river, we knew there was hope for the Nipintuk; our
expedition had been a success after all. You can well
imagine our relief - our sense of deliverance - the next
day when Indian summer arrived and stayed for a
week. In the shirtsleeve weather, the ice melted and the
Winneanimus ran chuck full of runoff from the hills! If
we'd continued our hike under the ice, we would still
have been en route; in that case, our fate would have

been anyone's guess.

Any speculation on that score was ended on the second morning of the thaw. Athabasca Jack and I stood watching the swiftly flowing Winneanimus and marveling at the sudden change in weather, when he clapped me on the shoulder and pointed speechless to a twisted mass of flotsam bobbing by in the river. Its splintered ends reached upward from the water like wildly clutching arms as it spun past us in the current. Jack and I exchanged sober glances that confirmed our recognition of the wreck: the shattered remains of the *Peapod.*

A PILGRIM'S PROGRESS

The booshway held up his hand for silence at the camp meeting. "Are there any announcements?" he called in a stentorian voice. He again gestured for silence as he scanned the crowd for buckskinners making their way to the center of the circle to shout their news.

Sidewinder and Ringtail had conferred under their breath at the edge of the crowd in the minutes preceding the call for announcements. The pair were often seen together at rendezvous, and they were not particularly esteemed for their character or neighborliness. Sidewinder was a self-styled blacksmith who would set up his portable forge in a central location and attempt to peddle his hardware. His nature seemed to be tempered with the brimstone associated with his vocation, and his rough ways and speech earned him few friends. His wares were likewise shunned by those in the know: his throwing knives frequently bent; his butterfly-forged tomahawks curled open at the seams or split their handles from end to end; and his fire steels proved barren of sparks after scant use. His products were undependable because they were the perfect reflection of their maker. He succeeded in selling some of them only because there are always a few uninitiated in the crowd, and because, with his brawn and his primitive dress and camp, he created a successful blacksmith image. Of Ringtail it had been said that he was the type of person who sometimes finds things before they become lost, and that he was so crooked that he slept on a corkscrew at night.

"Last call for announcements!" roared the booshway. As people turned away from the meeting, Sidewinder elbowed his way through the crowd and took up a position on center stage.

"Harken up, Pilgrims!" he bawled. He whistled

through his fingers and many buckskinners returned to the meeting ground to hear this last announcement. Sidewinder turned a full circle in the center of the ring to address everyone present. He gestured dramatically with both arms, pounding his chest and pointing to the sky; the long fringe, tin cones, and shells that adorned his war shirt amplified his agitation as he addressed the crowd in an imperfect imitation of Crockett's famous speech to Congress: "Hear me! My name is Sidewinder. I am half horse, half alligator, half tornado! My father was a lightning bolt and my mother was a she-cat! I am some! I can out-ride, out-shoot, out-run and out-rassle any man in this camp, and I aim to prove it! Meet me here at dusk and I'll rassle all comers on a bet. Remember to bring your wampum!"

The crowd seemed appropriately amused and turned to leave for individual camps. A few men lingered, talking in small groups and occasionally gesturing toward Sidewinder as if sizing him up for the challenge. Among the curious was a young pilgrim named Robin who was attending his first big rendezvous. He was anxious to take it all in and he was diligently exposing himself to as many facets of the experience as he could. Robin's athletic frame was covered by a simple calico shirt and new buckskin leggings. They were so clean that he stood out as a novice among the grizzled folks who surrounded him. His clothing and sparsely furnished camp marked him as a pilgrim, but his trim and sinewy torso hinted that with experience, he could become a real bull of the woods. Robin noted Sidewinder's challenge and he made a mental note to be present to watch the contest.

Sidewinder and Ringtail exchanged knowing glances and strode back to their camp together. As Sidewinder thoughtfully turned the handle on his forge to resuscitate the fire, he reviewed the details of his plan with Ringtail, glancing left and right to be sure no one was listening.

"You see, we'll set 'em up today and clobber 'em tomorrow. I'll make a pretty good showing at the rasslin' match tonight, but I'll let some pork-eater beat me a-purpose at the end. So we'll have to pay out tonight, but tomorrow I'll win us a foot-race and we'll collect it all back two-fold, 'cause folks will think I'm nothin' but a blow-hard and bet twice as much!"

"But what if you lose tomorrow too?" asked Ringtail, skeptical of his associate's plan. "After all, you're only exposin' yourself to the physical trials; I'm the one that's bankrolling this venture."

"Now, relax on that score, Ringtail. I might not be the strongest rassler in camp, but I believe I can run the fastest race. Why, I was watching a bunch o' 'skinners playin' lacrosse today and there weren't one of them I couldn't beat a-runnin'. I got long laigs and strong wind; if'n things gets tough, I could even use some of my pretty-good rasslin' tricks during the race. Stick by me, companyero, and tomorrow night we'll double our plunder." With a final, energetic turn of the forge's handle, the coals again glowed bright red.

At sundown, a fair crowd gathered at the appointed spot. Robin watched wide-eyed as Ringtail collected bets from the spectators and as Sidewinder and his first opponent warmed up on opposite sides of a circle inscribed on the ground with a stick. Sidewinder bellowed so half the camp could hear. "Waugh! Ringtail, you got the loot collected yet? I'm dyin' to lay my hands on this-here pork-eater! Stand back, everybody! Clear out the women and children! The sparks is gonna fly! Say, what's your name anyway, pilgrim?" he yelled to his opponent.

"Wild Turkey's the name and I'm from the Province of Maine! I'm king of the north woods! I'm the bare-handed logger! I break the pines off at the roots and skid the trunks out under my arms! And I'm ready to do the same to you!" It was plain that the challenger was game and that the match would be a good one. The spectators hooted their approval, some no doubt hoping to see Sidewinder get a good thrashing.

"Wild Turkey, you say? Well, your showin' up to rassle me proves that *half* o' your name is right. I know about you Mainiacs - got *tater* skins tacked up to dry on the barn walls to make into shirts and pants and such. Well, Ringtail, let the show begin! I got a hankerin' for some turkey, and I'll save ye the wishbone! Waugh!"

With that, Sidewinder pounced for his opponent and attempted to clasp him in a bear hug. But Wild Turkey broke the hold and turned the tables. Time and again the wrestlers changed advantage, up, down, and through all points of the improvised ring. The spectators cheered and whistled as the evenly matched combatants alternately staggered to their feet and threw each other to the ground. Frequently the onlookers had to scramble out of harms' way as flailing arms and legs overshot the ring's boundary. At one point, a tiring Sidewinder held Wild Turkey immobile as both tried to catch their breath. Sidewinder managed to pant for the benefit of the spectators, "Hey, Ringtail, it's time for me to put this man away. I hope you remembered to ask him his next of kin before we got started!"

But Wild Turkey exploded with a burst of energy and spun in Sidewinder's grasp so that they knelt facing each other in a crushing embrace. The one tried to stand up while the other exerted all his strength to haul his opponent to the ground. Sidewinder's efforts slowly prevailed as he forced the pair to their feet, a bizarre, grunting two-backed beast rising from the earth.   Sidewinder felt himself getting carried away with the match and thought to himself, "By Tunket, I've got to save myself for tomorrow; I better let this feller put me away and be done with it." So he relaxed an instant and Wild Turkey was quick to seize the advantage; he stepped behind Sidewinder and threw him over his hip, slamming him to the ground. Wild Turkey had put all his strength into the move, expecting more resistance, and Sidewinder was visibly stunned by the impact.   In a flash, the victor pounced onto Sidewinder's chest and pinned his shoulders to the ground. The crowd whistled and shouted their appreciation as Sidewinder climbed painfully to his feet and acknowledged defeat.

"Pay the people their money, Ringtail - this brute's done hurt my neck and knee so I can't rassle no more tonight." A jubilant Wild Turkey flapped his bent arms back and forth and gobbled loudly as he strutted in front of the spectators. His supporters clapped him on the back and congratulated him as they headed back to their camp. After the settling of the accounts, the contented crowd dispersed and made their way to various campfires for the evening's entertainment and socializing. Sidewinder leaned on Ringtail and limped conspicuously back to their camp.

In the privacy of their lodge, Sidewinder confided to his fellow conspirator, "Sufferin' Jehosaphat! I didn't think that pilgrim was gonna abuse me like that. You paid out some plunder tonight, amigo, but believe me, you got out of this one easy. Well, no matter; tomorrow I'll be good as new. The important thing is that it worked. We're on target and tomorrow we'll take them pilgrims for a real ride. 'Cause I know practically everybody in camp, and there ain't a soul that can pull foot faster'n me!"

The next day at camp meeting, Sidewinder again claimed center stage to reiterate his challenge. He still limped and his knee was bandaged ludicrously on the outside of his leggings for all to see. He intentionally addressed the crowd in a more subdued fashion in order to inspire confidence in potential challengers: "Now last night, as you know, I kinda had some bad luck and lost my balance in the rasslin' ring. But I'm *still* some and I'll prove it at two o' clock sharp today. I'll meet all challengers here for a foot race twice around camp. Remember to bring your wampum!" The other buckskinners chuckled, and the murmuring grew so loud as Sidewinder limped back to the circle, that the booshway had to call once again for silence.

At two o' clock, a group of curious spectators and a dozen challengers converged at the starting line. The course - two full laps around camp, including some ups and downs - amounted to about a half-mile. As on the previous day, Ringtail collected bets, and he shot intense glances at Sidewinder that revealed his intermingled avarice and anxiety for the outcome of the race. As the runners lined up, Sidewinder removed his knee bandage and boasted to his competition: "Soon as that startin' gun sounds, you pilgrims move to one side out of the way, 'cause I'll be steppin' up right smart behind ye at the end o' my last lap!" A dozen voices answered with taunts and jibes; only one contestant seemed too preoccupied to join in the verbal banter. Robin, the pilgrim, continued his warmups to one side of the crowd, a serious look on his face.

Ringtail stood to the side and in front of the starting line with his flint pistol raised. "Runners, get set ..." His tone of voice led them to believe that another command would follow, but he instantly pulled the trigger, to the surprise of nearly everyone. Among the contestants, only Sidewinder was in on the ruse, and off he dashed at the first flash. Robin was the only runner who wasn't caught flat-footed, and he sprinted off the line even with Sidewinder. But the pistol had only flashed, and the spectators and runners called for a restart.

"Pick that vent, Ringtail," called Sidewinder aloud, back at the starting line. The glance he shot at the starter said far more, though: "You incompetent! Now you've ruined the start!" An anxious Ringtail glanced in alarm at his cohort and at Robin; but Sidewinder narrowed his eyes and twitched the corner of his mouth in the general direction of Robin, leading Ringtail to understand that there were ways to deal with the young upstart.

When the pistol fired, the men were ready, and a pack of five runners stepped out for an early lead. Sidewinder was in the middle, and when he judged that the spectators' vision was obscured by intervening lodges, he gave a hard elbow to the ribs of the runner on his right. The runner protested and tried to keep the pace, but dropped back, panting unevenly. The leaders had dwindled to three as they began the second lap. As Sidewinder neared the point of his first infraction, he quickly crowded another runner too close to the guy ropes of a wall tent. The hapless runner successfully hurdled the first rope, but tripped on the second and crashed headlong onto the others, bringing down the entire tent with a great clanging of pans, splintering of poles, and rending of canvas. An irate camper emerged from the wreckage to protest vociferously and gesture wildly at the abashed and vanquished runner. Silently Sidewinder cursed the disaster, for now his foul play would be evident to all.

With two hundred yards to the finish, it was Sidewinder a half-stride ahead of Robin, who had been adroit enough to avoid the blacksmith's dirty tricks. He was also a stronger runner than Sidewinder had bargained for, and now both men made a desperate dash for the finish. As Robin moved to pass Sidewinder, the blacksmith swerved to the side to block his way. Robin chopped his stride, but not in time, as he accidentally stepped on Sidewinder's heel and sent him sprawling into the dust. Robin hurdled the tumbling form and crossed the finish line first, immediately turning around to see the fate of his fallen opponent. Sidewinder got to his feet, spat dirt, bellowed in protest, and stamped his feet with rage. At the finish, he cried foul and accused the young runner of intentionally tripping him. A dismayed Ringtail tried to call for a rematch on the next day, but the spectators protested, having learned of Sidewinder's low tricks on the distant end of the course. The will of the crowd prevailed, and once again, Ringtail was forced to pay out.

Robin headed back to camp, looking forward to a good sweat bath in the lodge by the stream. He was pleased with the win and regretted only that it had not been a clean one. Suddenly, he felt a rough hand grab his shoulder and spin him around. "What's yer name, pork-eater?" a vicious and still breathless Sidewinder demanded.

"I'm Robin. I didn't mean..."

"Robin! What the devil kind o' name is that? If that be yer rendezvous name, it's a pretty sissified one, and if it's yer real one, you better get yerself a rendezvous name, pilgrim. You better make it a good manly one too, if you want to avoid a lot o' hassle. And take this from me: don't cross me again or there'll be hell to

pay."   Sidewinder released Robin with a shove and
turned for his camp, still seething at his defeat.   He
knew camp life with Ringtail wouldn't be pleasant.

Ringtail and Sidewinder commiserated in their
lodge.   "Why that mangy son of a sea-serpent!" the
blacksmith growled.   "I'd a had him easy at the finish
if the varmint hadn't stepped on my heel.   There goes
our winnings and now it's gonna be hard to horns-
woggle them skinners into bettin' again.   I swan I've got
some bad luck with the birds, losin' to a turkey and a
robin back-to-back."

The loss festered for the remainder of the day.   As
Sidewinder worked at his forge, he was in an unusually
ill temper. He attempted to fashion a horse's head on
the handle of a fire poker, but he was too preoccupied
to carry it off.   "Heck, look at that mess!   I can't do
nothin' right today! The nose came out too long - looks
like a blasted bird beak." He held up the piece of iron
and looked it over.   "Heck, I wish to be shot if that don't
look like a dad-blarsted robin's head!   Robin!   Here, I'll
fix you," he muttered as he plunged the aborted form
into the coals and cranked furiously.   He withdrew the
poker at almost a white heat and placed the end on his
anvil, where he smashed the head into a formless mass
and tossed the scrapped project into the treetops with
his tongs.   "Take that, Robin, you bird-brain!"   Birds
fluttered out of the branches as the iron bounced off of
them.   "By Tunket if there don't be a whole cavvyard o'
robins all around here! Go on! Don't let me see no more
Robins flittin' around here!"   The exasperated blacksmith abandoned his forge to take solace in some
'shine.

After a session in the sweat lodge and a good
dinner, a much refreshed Robin set out for the camp of
some new friends.   This was to be his first trading

mission at the rendezvous, and he hoped to barter for some skins before the socializing began. To that end, he brought along some of his plunder: a pair of powder horns and possibles bag in one hand, and in the other, a wooden box containing some trade silver and beaded rosettes he had made. He still needed to pack a twelve inch cast-iron skillet in which a friend had expressed an interest. For lack of a free hand, he tucked the skillet handle down into his belt, closed his capote over it, and secured it with his sash.

As Robin wended his way through the camps, he stopped now and again to chat and listen to music. Eventually his path took him past Ringtail and Sidewinder's lodge, which was centrally located and hard to avoid. Robin hoped to slip past unnoticed, but he was accosted by Sidewinder and drawn over to the blacksmith's area. Hot coals still glowed menacingly in the forge.

"Listen, pork-eater, you put my tail in a mighty big knot with yer cheatin' ways! I think you're lower 'n a snake's pizzle!" Sidewinder tottered slightly and Robin could smell strong fumes from the 'shine on the blacksmith's breath. "I could run you out o' here. You better walk easy in this camp, or I'll torch yer lodge." This last was pronounced in a sinister, confidential tone. Ringtail remained seated on the ground on the other side of the forge, watching with amusement and doing nothing to defuse the mounting trouble. "Well, son, what you got to say fer yerself?" demanded Sidewinder.

Robin began to protest his innocence, diplomatically at first. But as Sidewinder grew more abusive, Robin decided the drunken ruffian couldn't be placated by civility, and that the only recourse was to withdraw. He tried to brush past Sidewinder, who

instantly bristled.   "Not so fast, pork-eater! I ain't
finished with you yet! Maybe I didn't show you that I'm
the strongest rassler or the fastest runner. But I know
for a fact that I've got the fastest one-two punch in
camp, and I'll prove it to ye now! Here, take this!"

"Wait!" Robin protested. But before the word
had cleared his lips, Sidewinder landed a swift combination punch hard on Robin's abdomen. A muffled
clang sounded above Robin's grunt. He staggered
backward and collided with the portable forge, which
crashed onto its side, spilling hot coals onto Ringtail,
who immediately bounded to his feet, screaming. He
bolted blindly into a rack of fire-irons and tipped over
Sidewinder's tool rack. The ruckus brought in buckskinners from surrounding camps, whose first vision
was Sidewinder bellowing in pain as he stamped about
holding his bruised fists between his legs. The intended K-O punch to the frying pan had taken the
liquor and the viciousness out of him. With his
antagonist so disarmed, Robin was free to make good
his retreat to a friendlier camp.

Robin's hosts noticed his agitation, and he was
prevailed upon to tell his tale. Afterwards, he traded
successfully for the desired skins. In fact, his friend
seemed to prize the skillet more for the role it had
played in giving Sidewinder his come-uppance. The
remainder of the evening was spent in good-humored
conversation and mountain music.

The following day, Robin sat shirtless in the
warm sun strumming his dulcimer with a goose quill
and noting with a chicken bone. He was still puzzling
over the events of the preceding day. Casually looking
up he saw with some alarm, that Sidewinder was
striding toward his camp, both hands bandaged.

"Howdy, pilgrim," began the blacksmith, while

still a good dozen paces away. "I don't mean to interrupt yer playin', but I wanted to talk to ye in the light o' day." He glanced down at the seated figure and noticed a pair of nearly concentric, skillet sized bruises that ran around Robin's midsection. "I reckon I got a little out o' hand yesterday. I had a little too much ridin' on the race, is all. It were my own doin'. Since we got another week o' rendezvous, I wanted to make peace. Ol' Ringtail, he's cooled down a mite today, too, but he hurts too much to walk on account o' where some o' them hot coals landed." Robin glanced toward the other camp and saw Ringtail, bowlegged and arms akimbo in his besmirched buckskins. Ringtail nodded acknowledgement to Robin, who nodded back. "Here, see if you can use this in yer kit." The blacksmith handed Robin a fire steel. "You might not want to depend on it if yer goin' out on a solo, aux aliments du pays. But you might could use it fer trade some time."

Robin was relieved to meet a subdued Sidewinder he hadn't known existed. He thanked the blacksmith and agreed that peace was the best policy. He commented that he'd been exposed to a lot and had a lot to absorb.

"Yep, I figger a feller with your spunk'll catch on right quick and turn into a prime skinner. You're likely to leave this doin's with a right proper rendezvous name too."

"Well, as a matter of fact, I got one already, Sidewinder. My friends had a little naming ceremony for me last night across camp."

"I wager it be somethin' like 'Lightfoot' on account o' the race. Am I right?"

Robin brightened and suppressed a smile as he stole a glance at the blacksmith's battered hands. "Not exactly. They call me *Anvil.*"

Eric A. Bye

BAT-EYE'S LAST LAUGH

Bat-eye and Iktomi had made an encampment on a level plain by a clear stream in the Catawampus Territories, where they intended to enjoy several weeks of trapping, hunting and fishing. Six hours in the saddle had brought them there from more civilized diggings, and though their aim was to subsist *aux aliments du pays*, they had brought their entire families, pets included. Bat-eye's cat had ridden the trail in a saddlebag and Iktomi's dog had trotted alongside his master's mount. The domestic animals entertained the children and cleaned up the scant leavings from meals and the day's catch. Game abounded, and edible plants rounded out the fare, so camp life was richer in some ways with all its strenuous requirements, than life back in the settlements. The group was usually a compatible one, with little more than Iktomi's occasional practical jokes to disturb their peaceful sojourn in Nature's lap. Iktomi's rendezvous name was derived from the legendary Indian prankster, for he often connived to execute some devilment at the expense of his companyeros. Bat-eye's cognomen was a reference to his nearsightedness and almost total dependence on his thick eyeglasses.

Bat-eye and Iktomi were returning to camp one day from a nearby hillside, where they had been practicing with their firelocks. Their conversation focused on the suitability of .62 smoothbores for major big-game animals, even dangerous ones. Bat-eye remarked, "Yup, with a fine firelock like this one, there's nary a critter in the woods a body's got to fear, exceptin' Ol' Ephraim, o' course."

"That be about right," rejoined Iktomi. "'Cause even without a gun, most times the critters will do their best to steer clear of us. Seems no matter how hard we try to disappear in the woods, every time we move we might just as well be drivin' through with a two horse threshing machine. But you know there's one critter in the woods 'at always gives me the heebie-jeebies, and I hope never to meet another jack one of 'em. 'Cause this varmint knows he's untouchable, and his medicine's about stronger than any other. Why he can drive you out of his haunts even after he's dead and gone, and the other critters give him all the room he needs."

"You talkin' grizz or painter or somethin' farther afield like an ice bear?"

"None o' them, ol' hoss. Try again."

"Gotta be wolverine or badger, then. Or rabid wolf. Like the one 'at attacked some o' the trappers at the Green River rendezvous back in '33."

"Nope. I'm talkin' *skunk*, pard. Them's the most inseedious varmints in the wild. I'll grant you they ain't mean like some, but they's so used to bein' left alone they don't even skedaddle if you stumble on 'em. You know, if you get sprayed twice in the eyes in your lifetime, you'll be stone blind for the rest o' your days. I warrant that's worse for me than for you, since you ain't so far from that now, haw! But I swan, you just can't imagine the agony of takin' a direct hit from a growed skunk. I got it once when I stepped over a log and practically trod square on the back of a record-book pole-cat."

"Waal, I don't wish that on ye," remarked Bat-eye, "but there's been times I thought it was fittin' enough treatment for ye. Like the time you pulled my tent stakes and the shelter fell in on me under the weight o' the snow. Wouldn't 'a' been so bad if'n I hadn't been naked as a jay bird and gettin' dressed. I won't forget that one right soon, so you better keep an eye on your back trail."

"Aw, come on, Bat-eye! I didn't do that, did I?

Why... Say, what was that? I thought I heard somethin' rattlin' around in the bushes. I tell ye, amigo, I'm so squamish about meetin' another skunk I keep hearin' 'em all around. You help me keep an eye peeled, Bat-eye; six eyes is better than two."

"Sure, there's plenty of skunks around here, Iktomi. Them devils lives everywhere. But how can you possibly run into trouble? You just gotta use your senses - any normal body ought to be able to see 'em or smell 'em ten rods off."

"Yep, but when I stepped on that one, I couldn't smell a thing for a headcold. Then I couldn't smell nothin' else for a week. You can't imagine anything like it, Bat-eye. I'd rather tangle with a painter than another pole-cat."

The two campers presently reached their camp and split up to do chores. Bat-eye sat down to lunch with his family. Then, feeling sleepy, he sent them on a mission to gather some cat-tail roots while he continued to nibble. Shortly he stretched out on his robes and began to snooze.

Iktomi soon heard Bat-eye's snoring; true to form, he concluded to pull a prank. He hadn't yet cleaned his smoothbore, so he loaded it with half a regular charge, but instead of a round ball he substituted as many dried elk droppings as he could find in the neighboring timber. Returning to Bat-eye's dooryard, he fired the blast into the open smoke flaps of Bat-eye's tipi, and shrieking a war-hoop, he ran around Bat-eye's tipi once before ducking into his own lodge. Bat-eye jumped up and stumbled coughing from his lodge. Iktomi called, "Say, ol' hoss, you all right? A party o' young braves just swooped down on our diggin's and tried to rustle our mounts, but they skedaddled when I come out of my tipi. One o' the rascals fired a shot into your lodge - I guess you heard it all right."

Bat-eye was not duped. He roared, "Can't you respect nothin'? I was gettin' my beauty rest, and now all that dust is rainin' down on my lunch leavin's and you know we don't got much to spare, livin' like this. You better hope I get this mess cleaned up before the rest o' the family comes back or you'll take the heat from the whole tribe. I should have known you'd be up to somethin' when my guard was down. I'm tired o' your prankin' around all the time. One of these days I'll think of a way to pay you back!"

Inside the lodge, the atomized elk chips were still filtering down. It was a futile gesture to clean up, and Bat-eye muttered imprecations as he tried to get the food under cover. It had always been a source of frustration to him that he couldn't devise an appropriate retaliation for his partner's tricks - a retaliation that was at once effective, satisfying, and less transparent than Iktomi's antics. But he resolved to even the score when the right moment presented itself.

Later in the afternoon Bat-eye's family returned with a good supply of wild edibles. His wife Morningstar and the children pitched in to start a venison stew. With the pot on to simmer and the dough for a galette all prepared, Morningstar arose from the hearth and announced her intention of taking the children for a swim at the river to clean up before dinner. "Bat-eye," she said, "I'll take care of this dough when I get back from the river. The galette will take only a couple of minutes to cook, and it's better hot, so I'll cook the batter just before we dig in. Just give the pot a stir now and again while we're gone."

Alone again in the lodge, Bat-eye continued to brood on a way to even the score with Iktomi. At that moment, the family's pet black cat purred and rubbed against his master's legs. The cat was seldom seen during the day, since he spent most of his time curled up on the robes; but now he was aroused by the smell of cooking food, and he hoped to bribe some from his human provider in exchange for affection.

Bat-eye absent-mindedly ran his hand down the cat's back to its thick Angora tail. A smile broke across Bat-eye's face as he recalled his earlier conversation with Iktomi and an idea dawned. "By Tunket, I've got it!" he muttered. "I'll fix that prankster once and for all. Cat, you varmint, you may be useless most of the time, but you're gonna do me a big service before the sun goes down. All you need is a couple o' white stripes down your back and you're the perfect counterfeit of a full-growed *pole-cat*. Hah, hah! Then all I do is sneak over to Iktomi's lodge when they're all in there havin' dinner, the dog included, and shove you into the scene." Bat-eye brightened and sat up straighter in his enthusiasm. "Let's see now... if I pull Iktomi's kitchen box over by the lodge door, I can stand on that and reach high enough to toss you in through the smoke flaps. Then plop! down you land, maybe right in somebody's chili, and the fun begins! There'll be heads bumpin' on the canvas and tin plates bangin' and the dog barkin' and carryin' on! Why there'll be a ruckus like a pair o' skeletons makin' love on a tin roof in a hailstorm, haw, haw! Then comes Iktomi flyin' out o' the lodge door head-first into the kitchen box that I forgot to move out of the way when I pulled foot to get back here. Ho, ho, I can see them plates and utensils scramblin' about on the ground now!

"But what in Tarnation am I gonna use for white paint? I know I don't got any in camp. Well, them stripes don't got to last too long; maybe I can use some flour and water mixed up into a paste." Bat-eye held the purring and unsuspecting cat in his lap while with one hand he reached for a tin cup and some flour from the galette project. He continued to stroke the cat while he prepared the paste. Then in a further flash of inspiration, he reached into the wicker pack basket he carried while tending his trap lines and pulled out a bottle of skunk scent. "We'll just add an element o' realism to your disguise, ol' Puss'n Boots!" And he poured a generous amount of the reeking musk into the white paste. "Phew! You'll be as good as the real item, Puss. You'll be unwelcome company for a couple o' days, but I'll make it up to you if you cooperate - you hear?"

Bat-eye continued to caress the cat, dipping his fingers into the fetid paste between strokes and applying it gradually to the cat's back. Presently the cat ceased purring; it began to blink and follow Bat-eye's hand with its gaze. Bat-eye tried to suppress the cat's squirmings as its tail flailed angrily and the other end tried to bite his hand. In the next instant, the combination of the smell and the moisture from the paste registered on the cat; he dug in his claws and sprang from his master's lap, instantly turning to lick the mixture from his back. Bat-eye sprang after the cat, hissing, "No, no, cat - leave that alone!"

The cat, now fully aware that he was being imposed upon, tried to flee; but not finding the lodge door, he began to sprint laps around the inside of the tipi. He bolted and bounded from plunder chests to backrests and bedrolls, knocking over sewing baskets and pots as he flew around the lodge, now high, now low. "Good, cat, that's the idea, but save it for the *other* lodge!" Bat-eye made a desperate lunge to catch the feline dervish for delivery next door, but the cat knocked over the uncapped bottle of skunk scent and bolted out the door into the falling dusk.

"Snaketurds!" hissed Bat-eye. "Get your mangy carcass back here or I'll string my banjer with you!" As he lunged through the lodge door to give pursuit, his face brushed the canvas door flap and his glasses flew from his head. "Well, I'll be dipped! How'm I gonna find them glasses without my wife or kids here to help? If I crawl around I'll just crush 'em myself, sure as shootin'. I better leave 'em where they lay and concentrate on gettin' my accomplice back in tow." Now without his glasses, Bat-eye could walk without getting hurt, since he could still perceive shapes and movement; but he was at a disadvantage at picking out details.

"Meow, meow! Puss, puss! Purrrrrr! Dinner time!" he called, trying to disguise his mission in case he was detected by the Iktomi camp. "Meow, meow! Here, kitty!"

Bat-eye made his way randomly trying to pick out any sign of the principal actor in his intended scheme. After a few minutes of searching, his path had led him several rods from camp. He heard a crunching in the leaves and detected a movement. An indistinct, squat form - mostly black, but with broad white stripes - was waddling away from him. "Hah! Gotcha now, you bugger! Come, kitty! Here, kitty! Whew, you really stink, cat! Maybe I overdid it with the perfume. Come, Puss! I want to introduce you to my friend, ho, ho!" The critter showed no signs of cooperating, and it even accelerated its retreat. So at the last instant, Bat-eye lunged to grab the fleeing form by the tail. "I'll get you, you flea-bitten OHGODHELPME!" he yelled in panic and agony as the real skunk scored a direct hit with a full charge. Gagging and sputtering and momentarily blinded, the daunted avenger staggered back to his camp. At a loss for a more effective remedy, Bat-eye grabbed a bar of soap and headed for the river. His instant reversal of fortune was as mortifying as it was painful; for in getting sprayed, the hopeful trickster had forfeited his revenge and set himself up for more guffaws from Iktomi. His plan had back-fired ignominiously.

Upon arriving at the swimming hole, he discovered that his family had already left, apparently taking another path back to camp. He peeled off his fetid clothing and prepared to dive in when he noticed that the fire pit by the sweat lodge was still burning. A good session in the initi - a cup-shaped canvas-covered wickiup with a pit for heated rocks in the center and room for a handful of people to sit - might steam the stench from his pores, and he chose that cleansing over a dip in the stream. He began to gather firewood to heat the rocks that would produce the billowing steam.

At that moment, back at the camp, Bat-eye's family was just entering their tipi. "Great God-a'mighty! What's happened in here? What a stench! Look, I see your pa's been usin' his nasty ol' skunk pee and spilled the whole bottle. Watch out! There's his glasses. What on earth's goin' on here? We'll have to eat outside tonight. I'll make Pa clean up this mess when he gets back. I'll have to cook up this galette quick and get out of here - I can't stand it. Here, Mandy, you take pa's glasses and go call him in. There, the rest o' you kids get out o' this stench - go round up your Pa or find somethin' else to do outside. Cough! He's gonna have some fancy explainin' to do by gum!" Morningstar's eyes watered as she grabbed for the skillet and galette dough. "Now what's this extra batter doin' in this tin cup? Must be one o' the kids took some out o' the trencher. Well, I'll just mix it all back in. Gosh! I can't

stay in here much longer!" And so saying, she kneaded
the cup of white paste into the galette batter and spread
it all into the skillet to cook.

Bat-eye in the meantime had approached the
tiny sweat lodge and heard a voice issuing from it.
Instantly comprehending that Iktomi was inside and
humming to himself, he brightened; his present discomfort wouldn't go for naught. Now possessed of
sufficient presence of mind to pursue his ruse, he
called to his partner through the canvas lodge, "Iktomi!
You in there? Open up. I want to come in for a sweat
bath."

"Aw, come on, Bat-eye. I've been a half-hour
buildin' up a good steam and if I open the flap now all
the heat'll get out. Why, a body can hardly breath in
here - it's jest perfect. Give me a couple minutes more
and it'll be all yours. Gasp! I can't stay much longer
anyway or I'll be cooked like a lobster!"

"All right, I'll wait." Then after a calculated
pause of a few seconds, Bat-eye yelled, "Iktomi, you
gotta open up! There's a big skunk hikin' through the
brush and he's headed this way! Move over, I'm comin'
in!" And Bat-eye slid under the canvas cover of the
sweat lodge. Instantly the overpowering skunk scent
filled the steam-laden air. Iktomi reacted by gagging
and scrambling in panic for the doorflap, thinking that
Bat-eye had let the skunk into the sweat lodge. But
Bat-eye was in the way and he held his ground; as
Iktomi grappled to get out of the thick atmosphere, he
became smeared with his avenger's sweat and the
hated reek. "Slow down, ol' hoss!" commanded Bat-
eye. "There's a big ol' pole-cat prowlin' around ten feet
from us and we've got to stay put till he leaves. No
skunk in his right mind would come into this steam;
this is the only place we're safe. Now, see, all your

thrashin' around must 'a' made him spray! But you can't go out or you'll get it again! Now let me splash some more water on these rocks; we gotta keep the heat up in here." Iktomi kept his hands clasped tightly over his eyes, and he fairly writhed in discomfort and anxiety inside the sweltering lodge. He had already been in the searing heat too long when Bat-eye arrived, and his body craved fresh air and cooler temperatures. Bat-eye, on the other hand, could easily last for another half hour. Periodically Iktomi would plead, "Bat-eye, open the flap an inch and see if that critter's still around."

"Sure enough pard, he's right over there. Why there's *another* one with him now; and I wish to be skinned alive if it don't look like they're preparin' to make a family! We can't interrupt that, Iktomi; we'd get it with both barrels for sure!"

As Bat-eye sprinkled more water on the rocks and a fresh batch of steam filled the initi, a panting Iktomi pressed tight to the ground, trying to avoid the heat. He squirmed, wiped the hot sweat from his body and doused himself with ladle after ladle of water. At last there was no water left in the lodge.

Finally Bat-eye was affected by his compa-nyero's agony and could himself stand the heat no longer.   Lifting the door flap for another look, he declared, "By Tunket, Iktomi, it looks like them critters has finally gone off for their honeymoon. I think it's safe to skedaddle."

A desperate and still gagging Iktomi grappled for the doorway, paused momentarily to scan the surrounding area, and plunged into the adjacent creek to cool off. In his subsiding panic, he failed to wonder why there was so little skunk scent outside the lodge - and no tracks - or how Bat-eye had observed the alleged skunks without the benefit of his glasses.

Bat-eye scrubbed down in the stream, exchanging comments with Iktomi about their near catastrophe, and headed back to camp, inwardly tickled at the success of his ruse. He had some serious excusing to do with Morningstar and the children, but he hoped they would share his satisfaction in the long-awaited vengeance on Iktomi.

Bat-eye still reeked, but was less offensive than before his sweat bath. He told his story and was not banished from the family. "I'm glad you finally paid Iktomi back in his own currency, Bat-eye," said Morningstar. "But I wish we'd known what was goin' on. You should have seen the confusion when the cat came home!"

"Well, I allow that wasn't quite how I'd planned to get even. But you'd 'a' been tickled to see Iktomi so flummuxed. He died a hundred deaths in that lodge; why, he was strung so tight on account o' them skunks that he would 'a' sweat bullets even if we'd been sittin' on ice cakes. I don't know what got to him most, the heat or the skunk smell. I swan I could almost see him glow red in the darkness of the lodge. Someday I might even rub salt in his wounds by tellin' him the whole story, but not until he promises to quit prankin' around all the time."

At dinner, Bat-eye ate heartily, though everything seemed to carry the taint of skunk. His family had abandoned the galette, complaining that it had absorbed too much of the stench from inside the tipi. "Well, I guess I worked up an appetite in all these shenanigans in spite of the smell," Bat-eye observed. "And I'm not one to sit around and watch good food go to waste." And so saying, he reached into the skillet and broke off another handful of galette.

THE TRACK OF THE WINDIGO

Sylvain Thibault was a life-long inhabitant of the northern woods, where a careful harvest of wild creatures for their meat and fur provided his modest living. Sylvain was born outdoors in the shade of towering hemlocks to a Waubanakee mother and an Awahnock (French Canadian) woodsman, and he was a blend of both cultures. His father's Catholicism and the spirits and legends of his mother's heritage were equal in Sylvain's consciousness. It was therefore consistent with his dual nature that on occasional journeys south to sell his furs, he would give thanks to a Christian God for a safe passage and make a tobacco offering to Wohjahose, the fearsome guardian spirit of Petowbowk, the *Lake that Lies Between.*

Sylvain tended a trap line stretching the length of the creek that ran by his rough-hewn cabin. Every morning in the Fall he would paddle as far as the stream allowed, collecting his furs and renewing his sets. Then he would beach his small canoe and continue by foot through the swamp that gave rise to the familiar creek and check some sets on another watercourse that issued from the distant end. Sylvain cherished the solitude of his work and the sense of independence and security it gave him. He felt that the entire wilderness area he knew as home was for his exclusive use. To be sure, he had no legal title to it; but years of walking softly on moccasined feet through the hospitable terrain, where the aggravations of civilization seldom intruded, had fostered in him a feeling of oneness with his surroundings that was so natural and deep-seated that he was reminded of it only when it was disturbed. He was thoroughly filled with the ethic and the lore of the northern wilderness; in Sylvain's mind, he belonged to the woods, and that was indistinguishable from the woods belonging to him.

On days of fair weather, Sylvain would often follow an indirect route back to his canoe. With his flintlock smoothbore in hand, he would scour the evergreen and alder thickets for partridge and woodcock. But just as frequently, his gaze would be directed downward, seeking buck sign that would be remembered when deer became legal quarry. One day on the eve of deer season, after a particularly long detour to check on some previously discovered scrapes, Sylvain returned tired and hungry to his canoe around sunset. He was glad to kneel for a while as he paddled; his legs needed rest from trudging over ridges and deadfalls. The water parted easily for Sylvain's canoe and gurgled musically as it rolled past the seams caulked with pine pitch; its motion was soothing, and Sylvain felt cleansed as he filled his lungs with the damp, cool air.

He had not paddled a half-mile downstream when a glint of fire light through the darkened forest arrested his alert and sweeping gaze. The light flickered with the intervening tree trunks, so Sylvain back paddled to watch and confirm his first impression. It was still there; the glint of campfire light was undeniable. Sylvain silently beached his craft once again and carefully stole through the short expanse of woods that separated him from the alien camp.

As he crouched in the shadows to survey the scene, he discovered a solitary camper tending a pot over the fire. Soon a companion stepped into the light from the other side of the fire and dumped an armload of firewood on the ground. The two campers spoke in English of an overturned oak nearby that could supply enough firewood to last them the week.

Sylvain judged that the fire was much larger than it needed to be for cooking, and that its tender had more enthusiasm than woods sense. He was reminded of an adage current in the culture that formed half his heritage: *Red man build small fire and sit close; white man build big fire and sit far away.* To Sylvain, that sentence summed up the two cultures and their differing approaches to the natural world, and spoke volumes about savvy in the woods and oneness with the wilderness. "*Sacre!*" thought Sylvain. "I don' need no *mangeurs de lard* trampoosin' t'rough my hwoods at de start of deer season!" Sylvain wasn't sure how to handle this intrusion, but he felt obligated to discover what the campers were up to.

After a moment, at a loss for a better way to introduce himself to the campers, Sylvain coughed loudly and strode into the firelight as the cook bent over the kettle to stir the soup. The startled camper dropped his ladle into the fire and his companion stood up so quickly from his log perch that he spilled half his cup of coffee.

"Salut, good evelin, gentermans. Don' be afraid of me. I seen you camp fire from ze water an' put in to be certain dere be somebody 'ere to tend it. Me, I don' take no chance wiz fire in my hwoods."

The strangers quickly recovered their composure, being relieved to discover that their visitor walked on only two legs and apparently bore them no hostility. Sylvain needed only a minute's observation to confirm his initial suspicion; the strangers were flatlanders who had come up to hunt deer, and many of the items in camp were too new to be well tried. One hunter's bright green and red plaid jacket and squeaky new boots, for example, appeared to be on their maiden expedition. Conversation revealed that the intruders intended to stay long enough to shoot a deer - for the entire season if need be.

Eventually one of the hunters slurped a spoonful of the stew boiling over the fire and proclaimed it fit for human consumption. He invited Sylvain to join them. The *coureur des bois* accepted readily, for his alternative was to paddle home on an empty stomach and start a meal from scratch in a cold cabin. Besides, he needed more time to figure out the two intruders.

"I guess we got fork stew instead of spoon stew," said one camper as he dipped a cup into the steaming kettle and poured the thick contents onto plates. As the other hunter rummaged through a pack for a third plate, Sylvain unsheathed his Green River knife and stripped a sheet of bark from a white birch log in the pile by the fire.

"Dat's all right," said Sylvain. "I got all da dish I need." And as he squatted by the fire, Sylvain scraped the stew from the rude plate into his mouth with his Green River. Sensing his hosts' amused gaze, Sylvain grinned while chewing and added, "Yas sir, hunger be da best seasoning, don't it? My meat bag sure emptee." When Sylvain was done, he wrung out his beard and wiped his mouth on his sleeve. Then he drew the knife twice across his thigh to clean it before returning it to its sheath. Finally, he threw his birch bark plate into the fire. As it curled and crackled, filling the camp with aromatic smoke, Sylvain remarked, "We don' want to leave dat layin' roun' in da night. You have porkypines or mebbe a bear come visit your camp and goozle up all da scraps and tear your camp apart."

The camper with the new boots seemed attentive and a little uneasy. "Are there many bears around here? Do you really think they'd come into our camp, Sylvain?"

"Wal, yas, if you leave food roun' and dere was bear nearby, he come in to clean up for you. An' if he still 'ungry, he come right in you tent, an' he not even knock, ho,ho! Sure dere be *plenty* bears in dese hwoods; you can hear dem 'ootin' in da Fall before dey get ready to sleep for da winter. Make sure to clean up good an' don' leave no food, *hein?* Hang dat kettly up 'igh in da tree branches if you don' want dat stew to call in da critters out of da hwoods."

The campers glanced at each other and took Sylvain's advice seriously. One carefully cleaned up the few dishes while the other secured the remainder of their food supply. Sylvain watched their earnest puttering and thought he detected a note of urgency and unease. He decided to test the two men a little more; though he appreciated the meal and the comfort of the camp, he was still annoyed at the prospect of sharing his woods on the morrow, the opening day of deer season.

With these few precautions completed, the men crouched in the fire light and talked hunting. Sylvain fished in a leather *gage d'amour* suspended around his neck and withdrew a coarse plug of tobacco, a part of which he whittled off and ground up in the palm of his hand. Then he filled the clay pipe he carried on the flap of his voyageur tuque and struck flint to steel to light it. Throughout this process, heat from the blazing campfire caused the overhanging evergreen boughs to rise and fall rhythmically like wings beating in a vain attempt to carry the trunks away from the fire. Under the starless sky, the dark seemed to squeeze tighter around the men until it became almost tangible. A cold wind made the plaid stranger shudder, and Sylvain noticed that his hosts seemed uneasy. "What you keep lookin' for out dere?" he asked. "Eyes shinin' back at you?"

"Naw, nothin' I guess. I just thought I heard something out there. Must have been the wind in the oak leaves. I reckon I'm just not too keen to meet a bear tonight, that's all."

"*Eh bien*, well, if you see eyes shinin' back at you, dat prob'ly no bear. Might be coyote or *loupcervier*, dough - you calls it painter, don't you? *Peste* !" exclaimed Sylvain as he drew the pipe from his mouth and inspected the extinct bowl.

As Sylvain reached again for his flint and steel, a companion offered, "Why don't you take a brand from the fire to light your pipe?"

"Bah gosh," answered Sylvain, "dat fire's too big to get a little stick from it widout I burn myself. Beside, dis way da best, ahnt it?"

"*Oui*," continued Sylvain between puffs, "dere be some pooty good deer in dese hwoods. You look roun' till you see da sign and follow dem to da deer, an' if you shoot straight you got him. But da land in here be pooty rough walkin'; jest be careful you don' step in no ol' well hole, hein? Back a couple 'undred year ago in time of Papineau dere was some farms in 'ere, an' da well 'oles still be roun' some times."

"I did notice a sunken hole not far from here when I was fetching firewood," rejoined one hunter. "I suppose that was an old foundation."

"Yas, dat was 'omestead. One time, Hinjuns come an' massacre families and burn 'ouses and barns an' keel settlers. Some says dere be fantomes still haunts dese hwoods at night. You don' might see dem, but mebbe hear dere voice in da treetops."

"You don't believe in ghosts, do you, Sylvain? I bet you spend more time in these woods than anybody else and you've never seen any haunts, have you?"

"Wal, no, dat be true enough. But I don' never disturb nothin' or go no place I don' belong, and I only take what I need to live. I *belong* here, by Gosh. I hear

tell dat fantomes don' bodder nobody dat don' bodder
dem. An' not everybody hear dem eider, bah Gosh. Dey
be 'eard only by dose dey *wants* to haunt."

"Then tell us, Sylvain, what they sound like so
we'll know when we hear them. Listen: hear those tree
squeaks in the wind? Is that what the voices are
supposed to sound like?"

Sylvain paused for a moment, listening. "Me, ah
don' 'ear nothin'; you better sleep wid one eye open
tonight." The glint in Sylvain's eye gave him away, and
the hunters chuckled at his attempted deception.

"Well, I don't believe there's anything in the
woods a grown man with a good rifle and a little
common sense needs to be afraid of," added one of the
campers.

"Dat's right, if you don't count Razor-shins and
loups-garou and lucivees and Windigo. You meet one
o' dem, you wish you never come to da hwoods, bah
Gosh. You take *loup-garou* for example; dey be evil man
sometimes in shape of man, sometimes like wolf or
odder animal. You meet *loup-garou*, you try to shoot
him or cut him wid you knife. If you draw his blood, he
turn back into man an' run away."

"How can you believe that baloney, Sylvain?"
asked the plaid camper. He glanced furtively at his
partner for moral support.

"I don' say I believe in dem or no," answered the
woodsman. "It's easy not to believe in dem 'ere in camp,
but when you gets way out dere in da hwoods, some
times you don' always t'ink da same way."

Sylvain puffed meditatively on his pipe as he
studied the reactions of his hosts. They had become
less talkative and gazed more intently into the fire,
occasionally glancing at one another. Sylvain continued his discourse, playing a hunch.

"But da worst of 'em all is da Windigo. You know, da people in da lumber camps be mighty tough men. But dey all afraid of Windigo. Only one man ever seen Windigo and live, an' he were Hinjuns." Sylvain gestured with his pipe: "Make sure you don' never cross track of Windigo or you be dead man. He's da terror of da North Hwoods."

The two hunters looked up at one another from the campfire. "How do you know the track of the Windigo, Sylvain?" asked the nervous one. The skepticism he forced into his voice belied his unease.

"You can't miss 'im. He walks lots like man. His foots be *gigantesques* , dough, prackly roun'; an' in da middle of every track dere be one drop o' blood dat hooze down t'rough his mockersons. If you ever see a track like dat, you turn and run away and never cross it or you be dead man!" Sylvain's conviction evidently produced the desired effect on the flatlanders. The hunter with the plaid jacket clutched his coat tighter around his neck and gazed intently into the fire. The light from the flames revealed tense movements in his jaw muscles and repeated, furtive glances into the shadows.

Conversation flowed less freely than earlier in the evening, and after a while, Sylvain knocked and scraped the ashes from his pipe. As he arose and stretched his weary body in preparation for the canoe trip home, he noticed that away from the fire the night had grown cold and held a promise of snow. "Dat's a good sign - mebbe we be lucky an' have good trackin' snow tomorrow." Then, explaining his need to paddle downstream to his cabin, he added, "I got to get some round balls for my fusil and finish skinnin' out my catch. You be up on first light in mornin' to hunt deers?"

"Yes, we hope to get a good early start. Good night and thanks for the information, Sylvain. If we don't meet in the woods tomorrow, good luck to you."

"Well, we prob'ly not meet tomorrow; dese hwoods so big we never find ourselve'.   Good night and *merci pour le diner.*"

Sylvain had taken only a dozen steps into the darkness when he was hailed by one of his hosts. "Say, Sylvain: one more thing. Have you ever seen anything that makes you believe there's such a thing as a Windigo?"

Sylvain paused a moment and answered thoughtfully. "Well, sir, I don' know. I never seen one. But it makes no different if I believe in him or no; I still be just as dead if I cross de track, so I don' take no chance wid it. An' don' you neider! *Bonne nuit,* gentermans."

As Sylvain crunched through the frozen leaves on his path to the canoe, a rising wind at his back carried snatches of the campers' conversation. They had just concluded to gather enough firewood to keep the campfire going all night. From the distance came the sound of two coyotes yipping and singing to one another.

Paddling downstream, Sylvain couldn't help feeling uneasy about the *mangeurs de lard* who had intruded into his woods the evening before opening day. He wished they could be encouraged to hunt elsewhere, and he was so preoccupied that the trip to his cabin seemed to last but a few minutes. As Sylvain beached his canoe, his breath frosted his beard and welcome snowflakes ricocheted like grains of salt off his face and hissed into the branches of the hemlocks.

Sylvain skinned a half-dozen muskrats by the light of his open fireplace after allowing them to thaw a little. As he peeled the skin from one of the carcasses, a drop of blood splattered onto the top of his moccasin. He paused an instant and a grin broke across his face as an idea dawned. "Aha! *Ca y est!*, Dat's it!" Then, humming snatches from "V'la le bon vent" he finished his skinning chores, squeezing and draining as much blood as he could into an oil can he kept in the cabin. The can was not altogether empty of oil, and Sylvain hoped the mixture would not coagulate. Setting the can near the fire, he tossed the carcasses outdoors for the coyotes and turned in with a self-satisfied chuckle. Sylvain had a plan. Bone tired though he was, the smile lingered on his face and it took him longer than usual to drop off.

A few short hours later, Sylvain jerked upright in his robes and cursed his sloth. The sky would soon begin lightening in the east, and Sylvain's exertions and late hours the previous day had caused him to oversleep. He would have to scramble to execute his plan in time; forced to forego his usual hearty breakfast, he hustled around the cabin to assemble his gear for the day's outing: rope, tomahawk, fusil with possibles, knife, lunch, a flask of rum, and his pack basket. Next he found an old pair of bear-paw snowshoes and laced some scrap hides onto each shoe to mask the web pattern. Then, grabbing his fusil and shouldering his pack basket, he strode out the door to his canoe. "Zut!" he exclaimed, returning at a trot to the cabin; "*Je ne dois pas oublier ca*; I almos' forgot da most important t'ing!" And tucking the blood-filled oil can into an inner pocket, he returned to his canoe.

The night had turned frigid and a layer of new, dry snow about three inches deep covered the ground. "*Tout va bien!* So far so good ef I don' be too late." Ice at the edge of the stream broke like glass as Sylvain pushed off and paddled toward the intruders' camp under a clear sky and a hunter's moon whose flat light cast everything in a silver hue. Sylvain shuddered in the cold until the exertion of paddling against the current warmed him.

A half-hour later, Sylvain beached his canoe and concealed it under a hemlock thicket. Then, picking his way carefully among the cover, he came in sight of the still burning campfire. He stole closer for a better look; seeing that no one was astir, he correctly concluded that the hunters had been awake longer than he the previous night, and that they were too snug in their robes to arise at dawn for the hunt.

"*Parfait!*" he muttered. Then, strapping on his modified snowshoes, he began to walk in a broad arc around the camp, stepping heavily with each pace. As he did so, he bent double to squirt a single drop of blood from his oil can into the center of each of the huge tracks. Burdened with his pack and possibles, stooping in the half-light of the pre-dawn morning, he cut a strange figure: a hunch-backed creature performing some slow-motion dance, silent and dreamlike. He described a semi-circle around the hunters' camp, over ridges and through swamps, a half-mile or so all told. The middle of the loop was at the stream and it opened in the direction from which the intruders had entered the woods. Sylvain was pleased with his ruse, but amusing though that was, he couldn't suppress a hope that his impersonation would escape detection by a real Windigo, if the legend had any basis in fact. He had no wish to antagonize so forbidding a creature as the Windigo, and Sylvain caught himself glancing warily into the deep shadows as he continued to lay tracks away from the camp.

"Now we see how long dey stay an' hunt," he chuckled to himself as he cached his snowshoes for retrieval at the day's end. Then he hiked off to begin his own day of hunting, glancing back several times to admire his handiwork and to be certain that nothing was yet astir within the horseshoe described by the fabricated trail. Sylvain's years of solitary habits had made him completely honest with himself, and he acknowledged relief at leaving the vicinity of the supposed Windigo and approaching his favorite hunting spot. His spirits rose in anticipation of the hunt, and an old tune he'd known all his life and which would not be denied sprang in a subdued voice from his lips:

> *Canot d'ecorce fut mon berceau*
> *Et la musique de mon enfance*
> *Fut le glouglou des eaux*
> *De la Nouvelle France!*

> *A birchbark canoe was my cradle*
> *And the music of my childhood*
> *Was the gurgling of the waters*
> *Of New France!*

Sylvain was on his stand shortly after first light. The day retained its bitter pre-dawn cold, accentuated by Sylvain's previous exertions, his fatigue and his immobility. He continued to reflect smugly on his ruse to purge the woods of the two outsiders, and he couldn't help wishing he could see their reaction to his trail. As the cold penetrated deeper into Sylvain's layered clothing, he took more frequent sips from his flask and chuckled with increasing self-satisfaction.

By mid-morning, the wind had mounted and the woods were becoming noisy. Trees groaned as they swayed, and squeaked where they chafed against one another; beech leaves shivered and hissed, and clods of snow crashed down through the hemlock branches. With such weather conditions, Sylvain became con-

vinced that few deer would be up and about. "Wal, if dey
don' be movin', I guess I better." As Sylvain stood up,
his head swam a little from sleeplessness and rum. He
acknowledged the effects of the anti-freeze in a body
deprived of breakfast and stepped cautiously as he cut
a winding trail back toward the camp, checking for deer
tracks on the ridges and in a swamp. In the swamp he
found a place sheltered from the wind by a stand of
gnarled evergreens. Now sleepy from drink and exertion, he shed his pack basket and planted himself on a
log to eat his lunch and rest his eyes for a few minutes.
In the ensuing half hour, enveloped in his blanket coat,
Sylvain enjoyed the delightful deep-woods slumber of
weary hunters. Shortly he woke shivering, and in his
temporary state of semiconsciousness, he remembered
only that his mission was to hunt deer. As he stood
uncertainly and began to stretch, he wasn't quite sure
where he was; as he glanced around, a yawn was cut
short as he noticed the cluster of withered pines that
formed his windbreak. "*Sacre*! Why I didn't see dat
before? Dat be a whole stand o' *bad luck* trees! *Sacre*!
No wonder I seen no deer 'ere. I got to get away from
'ere!"

Sylvain's aversion to unlucky trees - always
scraggly evergreens - was another common reflection of
North Woods superstitions. Tales abounded in lumber
camps of murders and heartbreaks, bad luck and
disappearances in the shadow of such trees. And
Sylvain had carelessly taken a nap a knife's throw from
a whole stand of them. Whether from the cold or his
aversion to the bad luck trees, Sylvain shivered as he
hoisted his pack basket and glanced uneasily about.
The camp of the other hunters was momentarily forgotten under the need to escape the influence of the
unlucky trees. Sylvain made tracks as quickly as he

could, and he felt his unease grow in proportion to his haste. His breath exploded in quick puffs and frosted his beard as evergreen branches rasped against his wicker pack basket and whipped him into hastier retreat.

Sylvain was nearly clear of the swamp when he rounded a thicket of alders and bamboo. He fairly shrieked as he inhaled, and stopped dead in his tracks: "*Putain!*" he stammered, crossing himself and turning to bolt in the opposite direction; for there in front of him, in a swath of smashed and trampled bamboo, was a set of tracks, fully two feet long, with a drop of blood in each one.

"Ohhh, ohhhhh," moaned Sylvain as he ran back, now totally disoriented. At the top of the first rise, he paused an instant to ease his heaving chest and glance back. Some unseen, large creature was crashing through an adjacent thicket, and its heavy breathing was audible even over Sylvain's.

"*Mere de Dieu!*" he yelled and bolted for level ground. He careened down the snow covered slope, barely keeping to his feet. At the foot of the ridge, an ancient logging road, still discernible, drew Sylvain along. He could still hear the crashing and panting hard behind him. Fifty yards more, and Sylvain was spent; too exhausted to lift his feet, he caught one in a root and slammed face-first into the snow. Upon impact, the contents of his pack-basket catapulted out the open top; a burning pain stabbed into the back of his head and shot down between his shoulders. In that moment, Sylvain feared the searing grasp of the Windigo. His vision swam as the pursuing creature plodded past him, unseeing, with a gait sapped by fatigue but driven by panic, each step accompanied by a rasping breath and a groan. As Sylvain swooned, his last vision was of a moaning, green plaid form stumbling blindly away from him.

Sylvain lay unconscious for an hour. When he finally stirred, he gave a start and made a move to jump to his feet. The pain in his head checked that movement though, and he sank to a sitting position. He held his aching head and discovered blood on the snow - his own. His tomahawk and other gear were scattered about. A minute patch of bloodied scalp stuck to his 'hawk hinted at the cause of his wound. Then his fleeting vision of a receding form clad in green plaid snapped back into his head, and he checked the tracks that led past the spot where he had fallen. The tracks were man-sized, and in fact the soles of the boots that made them showed scarcely any wear. The pieces were starting to fit together.

Cautiously, Sylvain stood up. Gathering his gear, he double-checked the tracks and laughed. "Ho, ho! *Succes total!* But by Gosh, I almos' fool myself, too! Dat man so afraid he don' even see me when he run by."

The hunter got his bearings from known landmarks and headed back to the stream. As he'd suspected, the camp was vacated, apparently in great haste. A bow saw, some matches and a lantern had been left behind, and Sylvain gladly gathered them into his pack. He hiked to the cache where he'd left his snowshoes, and then retrieved his canoe.

Back at the cabin, Sylvain grinned. "My trick almos' work too good. But dose dam' bad-luck trees is what set me off. I'm lucky all I got to show for dat foolishness is a little cut on da head. I ahnt seen much deer sign all day, but a lantern an' a saw ahnt bad for a day o' ramshackin' t'rough da hwoods. An' tomorrow be da start of da rest of da season in my own hwoods, an' all by myself, by Gosh!"

PICKBONE'S VICTORY
DASH

Through two days of demanding competition in mountain-man skills, Pickbone and his friend and arch-rival, Apple Jack, were neck and neck. The stakes were high - a custom made flint rifle with matching horns and possibles bag - and the outcome would be decided by the day's remaining events: the flint-and-steel fire-start and the hunter's run. Apple Jack wasn't known to be the most scrupulous competitor, especially when he was vying for prime plunder, so Pickbone should have been on his guard when Jack invited him over for lunch before the final events.

"Smells mighty good, Jack. My meat bag's plumb empty after this mornin's shootin'. Right decent of you to have me over to share your kettle. What you got cookin'?"

"Why, come right over and sit down, Pickbone. Man alive, you're lookin' just as ugly as ever; but it won't do you no good, you can't scare me! Mighty fine to have you here, ol' hiveranno. Here, pull up a stump next to the fire. I cooked up my favorite eats: pea soup to start, and my special baked beans, sauerkraut and Jerusalem artichoke casserole. Here, dig into a good mound o' these vittles so you'll be strong enough to beat me this afternoon."

"Whoa, Jack, I can't put away all that!"

"Now come on, Pickbone! You can't come into my camp and refuse my hospitality. You gotta uphold your reputation as a mighty wielder of a fork! I spent a lot o' time fixin' this chow for you, and it's all good, authentic pioneer food. Pack it in now, you know it's a long time till supper, and you don't want to insult your kind host. Naw, don't worry about me friend," he protested, "I already had mine. In fact I was just finishin' as you came up. See, there's my plate. Here, wash that down with a quart of my home-made brew."

Just as Pickbone forced down the last of his beans with a sigh of relief, Jack piled another round onto his plate. "Come on, ol' hoss, you gotta help me finish this stuff; you know it won't keep." Jack wouldn't take no for an answer, and a while later when the pots were emptied and Pickbone stood up to thank Jack for the meal, he felt bloated and logy.

"Jack, I'll see you at the fire start. I gotta round up my possibles and get ready. That was a fine feast for sure. I might of et a little more 'n I needed, but that don't matter; I'm still fit as a fiddle. Thanks for the feed and good luck this afternoon; you'll be needin' it."

"Good luck to *you*, Pickbone," Jack grinned back.

By noon the day had turned hot, so when Pickbone returned to camp to retrieve his possibles, he decided to change into his breech-cloth for the last two events of the aggregate. Even as he walked back to his shelter he could feel the mounting distention produced by Jack's meal. "By Tunket," he muttered, "maybe I should have gone easier on them vittles after all."

"Now where in God's green earth did I leave the sash for this-here breech-clout?" muttered Pickbone as he ran his hand over his swelling paunch. "Well, no matter; I'll make do with this old piece o' rawhide thong instead." Grabbing his rifle, possibles and fire kit, he ambled uncomfortably over to the fire start.

Several competitors were ahead of Jack and Pickbone, and by the time Jack took his turn at making fire with flint and steel, Pickbone was experiencing severe abdominal discomfort and rumblings. Jack had flames in nine seconds - a respectable time, but one which could be beaten. He stood up brushing tinder from his beard, and crushing the small fire with the heel of his moccasin. "Show us how it's done, pard!" he grinned at Pickbone.

Pickbone knelt to strike sparks to char-cloth. His abdomen resented the added compression and objected with a sound akin to that made by dropping a large boulder down a deep well. He appeared very uncomfortable and beads of sweat began to appear on his forehead.

Pickbone's tinder resisted his continued efforts to blow the sparks to flame. His char-cloth was nearly consumed, and he waved his bundle of tinder in the air between breaths; in his smoke-reddened eyes Jack read the distress that had two causes: the damp tinder and the intestinal discomfort from the meal. As Pickbone puffed harder and harder in a frantic attempt to kindle fire before time ran out, his intestinal gurgling topped with a crescendo, until with a final, but futile, breath, and to his instant and lasting mortification, he fairly rent his upended breech cloth with an irrepressible, flatulent eruption. "You oughtta hold that tinder behind ye!" yelled a spectator, and all present, especially Jack, dissolved into laughter as the last grains of sand trickled through the timing glass. Pickbone had missed the fire start.

After that event, Jack had a small lead, and Pickbone knew he'd have to perform well on the hunter's run.   Both friends were equal with the rifle, and Pickbone figured he'd need to pick up points for time. Jack was thinner and more fit, though; and as Pickbone now realized, Jack wasn't carrying a cargo of gaseous vittles in his paunch.

On the hunter's run, the first shot was taken prone behind a log, firing at buffalo silhouettes. Jack toppled his and lit out lickity-clippity with a war-whoop for the next firing station.

Seconds later, Pickbone lay down for his shot in

full view of the spectators. He winced once again at his swollen paunch as yet another boulder plummeted into the depths of the well. Despite his discomfort, he shot center and his target fell with a delayed clang. Up he sprang with a victorious hoot to dash away to the next firing point. But in sprinting from a crouch, he accidentally stepped on the front of his breech-cloth and popped the aged rawhide lace that held it in place. Four strides later, he comprehended his predicament; skidding to a halt, he reversed directions to retrieve his fallen breech-cloth. But instantly he saw that it was farther to the breech-cloth and the guffawing spectators than to the protection of the alder thicket through which the trail ran. So back he charged, his smooth moccasins slipping on the grass under foot. Pickbone knew he needed every second he could save as he dashed along the trail into the thicket, clad in the most primitive outfit ever witnessed on the range.

For the next few minutes, both contestants were lost from sight. Spectators judged their progress from the reports of the rifles and knew when Pickbone reached Jack by the mixture of haw-hawing and heckling that issued from the brush. Momentarily there came a shot followed by a whoop, and Pickbone emerged first on the distant end of the return trail. The crowd cheered as he galloped hellity-toot; and what a figure he cut! Face bright red from exertion and embarrassment, he attempted to maintain his dignity by holding his possibles bag in front as he ran. Past the spectators he ran, puffing like a steam locomotive both fore and aft, and fairly tooting "Yankee Doodle". He drew his tomahawk and threw it to the mark without breaking stride, ending his time for the run. Without pausing, he continued his sprint back toward camp and missed seeing Jack's finish nearly a minute later.

Eric A. Bye

The scoring showed that Jack and Pickbone had hit all targets. But Pickbone had gained enough time to win by a point.

"That was a fine run, Pickbone," Jack admitted later. "I never seen you run so fast. I thought your new rendezvous name was gonna be 'Breaks-the-Wind'. But I still think I would have beat you if I hadn't been so distracted by you runnin' up on me in your natural skins that I dry-balled my rifle."

"Jack, I couldn't have run like that just to beat you. I needed to hurry back to heed the call of nature. That was *almost* a prime trick you played on me, tryin' to keep me off the mark by rilin' up my innerds. But I reckon I owe you some thanks, for without your help I wouldn't have needed to run fast enough to win this here fine rifle and possibles."

The Author in His Study

Eric A. Bye is a native of New England who has lived most of his life in Massachusetts and Vermont. He has an MA in foreign languages from the University of Vermont, with a specialization in French language and literature. He has had an interest in antique guns and buckskinning since childhood, when he was captivated by the Davy Crockett legends. He has a deep interest in writings from and about early America, including frontier humor. He builds his own muzzle-loading rifles and was booshway of the 1989 Northeastern Primitive Rendezvous.

Eric currently resides in Saxton's River, Vermont with his wife and two children. He enjoys alpine and cross country skiing, competitive smallbore rifle shooting, playing the banjo, and bicycling.

Acknowledgements

Special thanks to Kris Sweat and Billie Jean Peterson for reading the manuscript and making suggestions. Brenda Martin proofed the manuscript and Jill Rensel added the color to the cover illustration. John Lippincott assisted by photographing the author. Thanks also to my editor, Denise E. Knight, for her assistance in going from manuscript to book.

Quote on Page 114, *The Ballad of Blasphemous Bill*, from Ballads of a Cheechako by Robert W. Service, Copyright 1909 by Edward Stern & Co., Inc.

Quote on Page 76, *The Buffalo Skinners* adapted from The Banjo Player's Songbook by Tim Jumper, Copyright 1984 by Oak Publications, a division of Embassy Music Corporation, New York. International Copyright Secured. All rights reserved.

An Exciting Adventure from Eagle's View:

A Circle Of Power

by
William F. Higbie

Bull Calf, a young Indian boy, stands on the brink of manhood as life among the Plains Indians, from a young adult perspective, unfolds. What he considers an education, we would call an **adventure** - for that's what it is.

As Bull Calf copes with the birth of a sister and the death of his mother, the time comes for him to "seek his vision" and receive his adult name - Otter Circle.

Buffalo hunts, his first horse raid, the confusion of first love and dealing with the taunts of Badger, a young bully, are all part of his passage into the adult world. Will he make his father proud and become a great warrior? Or, will his young life end in battle, his scalp hanging from an enemy lodge pole?

Well written and simply told, this story goes beyond the boundaries of time and place as Bull Calf learns about feelings with which all young people must come to terms. The book helps dispel the Hollywood cliches of the noble savage and the blood thirsty barbarian, and avoids "Tonto talk" as it provides a well researched description of Native American life on the Plains prior to the arrival of the white man. All this within a narrative which is packed with excitement and hard to put down! You and your children won't want to miss this book.

SOME EAGLE'S VIEW PUBLISHING
BEST SELLERS THAT MAY BE OF INTEREST:

• •

The Technique of Porcupine Quill Decoration
    Among the Indians of North America
      by William C. Orchard (B00/01) $8.95
            In Hardback (B99/01) $15.95
The Technique of North American Indian
    Beadwork by Monte Smith (B00/02) $9.95
            In Hardback (B99/02) $15.95
Techniques of Beading Earrings by Deon
    DeLange (B00/03) $7.95
More Techniques of Beading Earrings
    by Deon DeLange (B00/04) $8.95
America's *First* First World War: The French
    and Indian War by Tim Todish (B00/05) $8.95
Crow Indian Beadwork by Wildschut &
    Ewers (B00/06) $8.95
New Adventures in Beading Earrings by
    Laura Reid (B00/07) $8.95
North American Indian Burial Customs by
    Dr. H. C. Yarrow (B00/09) $9.95
Traditional Indian Crafts by Monte Smith (B00/10) $7.95
Traditional Indian Bead and Leather Crafts
    by M. Smith & M. VanSickle (B00/11) $9.95
Indian Clothing of the Great Lakes: 1740-1840
    by Sheryl Hartman (B00/12) $9.95
            In Hardback (B99/12) $15.95
Shinin' Trails: A Possibles Bag of Fur Trade
    Trivia by John Legg (B00/13) $7.95
The Hair of the Bear by Eric A. Bye (B00/20) $9.95

• •

Adventures in Creating Earrings by
  Laura Reid (B00/14) $9.95
A Circle of Power by William Higbie (B00/15) $7.95
  In Hardback (B99/15) $13.95
Etienne Provost: Man of the Mountains by
  Jack Tykal (B00/16) $9.95
  In Hardback (B99/16) $15.95
A Quillwork Companion by Jean
  Heinbuch (B00/17) $9.95
  In Hardback (B99/17) $15.95
Making Indian Bows & Arrows ... The Old Way
  by Doug Wallentine (B00/18) $9.95
Making Arrows ... The Old Way by Doug
  Wallentine (B00/19) $4.00
Eagle's View Publishing Catalog of Books $1.50

• •
At your local bookstore or use this handy form for ordering:
• •

**Eagle's View Readers Service, Dept HOB
6756 North Fork Road - Liberty, UT 84310**

Please send me the titles listed. I am enclosing $_____
  (Please add $2.00 per order to cover shipping and
  handling.) Send check or money order - no cash or
                C.O.D.s please.

Ms./Mrs./Mr. _____

Address _____

City/State/Zip Code _____

Prices and availability subject to change without notice. Please allow three to four weeks
for delivery. (HOB 10/90)

American Indian Culture from Eagle's View:

North American Indian Burial Customs

by
Dr. H. C. Yarrow

edited by Dr. V. LaMonte Smith

This informative and interesting book was written for the Smithsonian Institute, Bureau of Ethnology, in 1879 while Dr. Yarrow was serving as the acting assistant surgeon general of the United States.

Based on personal research by physicians in the field and all other available primary sources, this book describes and illustrates in great detail the burial/mortuary customs of all the major Indian Nations and the ceremonies pertaining to these practices.

Mortuary customs, including inhumation (burial in the ground), deposition of remains in urns, embalmment, surface burial, cremation, aerial sepulture (box, scaffold, tree and house burial), and aquatic burial are described in explicit verbage and with first hand authority. The contributors are very candid about any personal bias; a refreshing change from the position of contemporary social scientists with their claim of "objectivity" and emotional distance.

This book will be invaluable to anyone interested in the traditions and culture of the American Indian. Well researched and fascinating reading.